THE ORPHANAGE FOR WORDS

Shinie Antony has written three books of short stories—*Barefoot and Pregnant, Séance on a Sunday Afternoon* and *Planet Polygamous*—and two novels—*Kardamom Kisses* and *When Mira Went Forth and Multiplied.* She has compiled the anthologies, *Kerala, Kerala, Quite Contrary* and *Why We Don't Talk.* She won the Commonwealth Short Story Prize for the Asia region in 2003.

Praise for previous books

'Shinie Antony has a distinctive understated style, black humour and quiet focus on the soul. A powerful writer and excellent storyteller, she serenely provides unusual, even bizarre, solutions to conventional wants. Readers of her books would be familiar with her fascinating view from the other side, the dry wit, the dysfunctional lives, the little eccentricities, the clawing desperation, the search for dignity of the devastated.'
—Antara Dev Sen, *DNA*

'If there's a literary equivalent to the minimalist artist, it is Shinie. She manages startling nuances with a juxtaposition, twist or unusual usage. Her characters reach the edge of expected behaviour only to go into a slew of surprises. With a few words she swiftly forges resonant implications.'
—Shreekumar Varma, *The Times of India*

'Shinie Antony is a gifted writer… has absolutely no interest in feel-good presentations.' —*The Hindu*

'The febrile edgy voice haunts the reader's imagination with a peculiar force of conviction.' —*Biblio*

'Antony's funniness is of a conspiratorial kind. It's personal, between you and her alone. Roll the lines a little over your tongue, let the wit seep in, and savour the aftertaste. This way you would've acquired a not-so-easily-satisfied taste for intelligent humour.' —*Deccan Herald*

'Often atrocious, often outrageous, often dark, but funny all the time.' —*The New Indian Express*

'Shinie Antony is brave enough to move away from the usual style of writing to create her own.' —*The Financial Express*

'Zany, inventive, sardonic, deliciously irreverent.' —*The Week*

'Sometimes moving, sometimes startling, sometimes unnerving and sometimes tragic.' —*Outlook.com*

'The lightness of tone is kept skin-deep as Shinie Antony takes us into worlds that are about to stop ticking.' —*IANS*

'A heady mix of slapstick and sadism.' —*India Today*

THE ORPHANAGE FOR WORDS

SHINIE ANTONY

RUPA

Published by
Rupa Publications India Pvt. Ltd 2015
7/16, Ansari Road, Daryaganj
New Delhi 110002

Sales centres:
Allahabad Bengaluru Chennai
Hyderabad Jaipur Kathmandu
Kolkata Mumbai

Copyright © Shinie Antony 2015

Page 180 is an extension of the copyright page.

This is a work of fiction. Names, characters, places and incidents are either the product of the author's imagination or are used fictitiously, and any resemblance to any actual persons, living or dead, events or locales is entirely coincidental.

All rights reserved.
No part of this publication may be reproduced, transmitted, or stored in a retrieval system, in any form or by any means, electronic, mechanical, photocopying, recording or otherwise, without the prior permission of the publisher.

ISBN: 978-81-291-3695-4

First impression 2015
10 9 8 7 6 5 4 3 2 1

The moral right of the author has been asserted.

Typeset by Saanvi Graphics, Noida

Printed at Thomson Press India Ltd., Faridabad

This book is sold subject to the condition that it shall not, by way of trade or otherwise, be lent, resold, hired out, or otherwise circulated, without the publisher's prior consent, in any form of binding or cover other than that in which it is published.

For Dad

CONTENTS

GIRLFRIENDS	1
A TALK	11
STATUS QUO	16
PLANS	28
HAIR	35
FATHERS	41
THE CRY	45
A MAN	53
KITE	66
THE FROCK	71
MORNINGS	79
BREASTS	84
DOG	99

HEARTS	**102**
DOLL	**115**
THE SOFA	**120**
SONS	**130**
NIGHTS	**142**
THE BITCH	**147**
HAPPY	**160**
DAUGHTER	**166**
WORDS	**169**
COPYRIGHT ACKNOWLEDGEMENTS	180

GIRLFRIENDS

They are here to act their age, not giggle and be silly. To mull the goodness of the good old days over reheated coffee. For falling madly in love and falling madly out of love, two types of madly as everyone knows.

He coughs. She looks up quickly, too quickly. Hope, a refined form of self-abuse.

I need common sense, she thinks desperately, as if ordering a drink. One Common Sense, please. On the rocks, with ice, lots and lots of ice. Because this is nonsense, what he says, what she will say. And who'll pay? She will, in big fat ugly sobs. Recession has struck romance, girlfriends are being given the pink slip. This is him going hmmm, the mercy-kissing.

Oh, she should just jump up and go over to where she recognizes someone sitting in a large laughing group. Back at her table is a lull. The silence draws her back into her body, which is 32-30-36, not bad for her age, 35. Okay, 40.

He puts arms behind head, stretches legs, and is all playful sloth. 'Ages, huh?'

As a child, a yawn or a laugh would lock her jaw with a click. Which meant long hours of not being able to close her mouth. Her father would come early from office and take her, bib and all, to the dentist who'd inject numbness in her chin and unlatch the mouth. Throughout that humiliating journey, with neighbours, other children and people in the clinic staring at her, at her unblinking, wide-open mouth, what she wanted to say—but couldn't with things the way they were—was: I am not laughing, screaming or amazed, this is not an expression of anything, alright?

She sits somewhat similarly now, with a look on her face not put there by her. As they order their coffees, she is not sure why she is here, why he is here. The liker likes the liked to like the like. Unrequited is a grand word, but a stalker and a sigher. A Shakuntala of a word, as if come what may, man fleeing or memory loss, I will go on. Couples should come fitted with walkie-talkies. When one says over and out, the other says over fucking out.

She places her mobile—with two prosaic messages from him: a) *free for coffee?* b) *just reached*—on the table between them. Inside her head, from habit, are stored up anecdotes to relate to him. But even as she opens her mouth he looks away, strums an imaginary guitar. She is a secret drummer herself. Wrists to the right, head thrown back, she plays better when she snarls.

They met at an HR convention abroad, where all rules seemed suspended, when they shared paranoia in the dim glow of jet lag and disorientation and sleeping wrong hours. They were never such avid listeners, never such avid talkers. On their sixth coffee from the same cup it was as if they just learnt to talk, to put words together. What made them laugh in the outside world ceased to amuse, what seemed normal until they met seemed inconsequential, for lesser mortals. A dead sibling, a bossy father, every desperation and personal humiliation came tumbling out of their mouths, stomachs, hearts and minds, confident of a hearing, of being understood, cleansing in its wake, leaving behind squeaky-clean insides so they felt like teeth in toothpaste ads, as if an oversized glint of light twinkled on them.

'Can you for once just pretend you are dead, that you don't know what's happening? That's the only way to go on,' she had flung at him protectively, wanting to shield him from himself, her spiritually dysfunctional twin.

'I will,' he said, 'if you kiss me.'

'Kiss?' she laughed. 'A proper kiss?'

A roguish, 'If not improper.'

No fan of her own face, she'd shrugged. 'If you can bear to look at my mouth for an hour.' Looked at her watch. 'Your time starts now.'

He said nothing, already watching her mouth.

She moved on to the podium where she, along with two grim women, held forth on sexual harassment during work hours. Her mouth, which she studied in mirrors every day, was sure to repel him on closer study. If not, well, anything goes under a foreign sky.

By the time she walked towards him she felt like she had always walked towards him. When their lips met it was speech in a strange new accent. The kiss ran up her feet like upside-down rain, wetting her toe to top. For months after she'd go on tiptoe at the thought of him.

That first night he whispered between her shoulder blades, 'I am impotent.' And thinking only how exquisitely matched they were, she said, 'I am frigid'. Frequently, at length, again and again, for the better part of three days, without much food, sleep or fresh air they proved each other and themselves, with uneven gasps of surprise, wrong.

He said the said thing, she did the done thing.

'That's what men tell women,' she scoffed, though what she wanted to do most was believe him implicitly. Pluck the words from his lips and lock them in her ears. She'd never known this about herself, that inside her was a desperate hobo rattling a tin for sweet nothings.

With husbandly casualness he flicks open his wallet and presents to her his wife. She leans forward to look at the pic for it's only polite; a plane takes off in one ear, lands in the other.

There is such repose and rest on the wife's face, such an unhurried acceptance of the camera's flash that one cannot have an opinion on her one way or another except accept the solidity of her existence. A lace dupatta in powder blue coming down a shoulder and some pet name he uses with calculated fondness.

In a world where marriages bruise and burst open like rotten fruits left too long on low-hanging branches, his own—he vows—is 'different, touchwood'. Wood will sue him one day, she thinks, as he looks around, locates and rubs reverently the leg of their table. Wood will come for him, one tree at a time, and saw off his lying tongue.

Doesn't he care that she will hunt for a cowering, tender-hearted heart and break it in two in her own turn? That many men and many women will go tumbling down the line for what he is doing to her?

She notices he is using her name a lot. A PR trick. She doesn't say his name once. From now on, all must be hidden. The book she read, the movie she saw, the dish she burnt. References to their joint past. Private jokes. The shape of her mouth as she says his name.

She is someone, he says, he shouldn't have met, someone he should have been able to resist. It's all her fault, does she know?

To be someone's moment of weakness, how ennobling! Her blood boils. Nonsense, her blood is just some boring B+ stuff minding its own business.

Words went away so soundless she didn't notice at first. We are getting used to each other, she thought, we are taking us for granted. She lived her life in a flat her friends praised for its funky doormats, poetic view and ridiculously high rent, and pretended his silence was a song only she could hear.

His was a self-absorbed silence more about him than her. Like the incessant babble of some who spoke solely about themselves, he didn't talk at all only out of self-importance. Not to get her attention. This was the genuine article, to give him his due; he had moved on. If only mobile phones had never been invented! Then she wouldn't know how much she was forgotten, how often he wasn't thinking of her. A silent phone clicks like a gun.

He had given her in the early eager days all his phone numbers; in fact, wrote them down himself on a piece of paper handed to her anxiously, not taking his eyes off her face. She has never called on any of these numbers—at his home, at his office… She just knows that if she ever did he would say hello-hello-hello as if he cannot hear her and she will say hello-hello-hello thinking he really cannot hear her and they'd both go down in a blaze of helloes.

She had howled, wailed, texted him her heart. Then she saw red, ready to courier him her middle finger. A sty in each eye, it was her year to cry. She dieted, shrank her body, got drunk, drew dark circles under her eyes. Astrologers said Saturn was here and, hey, an entire planet to blame.

She watches him sip his coffee. Why hasn't she noticed this before? Bed-wetter eyes, a chin incapable of beard and hair not enough to fit the head. Should she, she thinks idly, fall at his feet and beg him not to leave her. After all, he may be expecting it, and she is not the type to disappoint anyone, especially not him, especially not until now.

He'd eat you in two bites if you let him, she scolds self. Being edible is a biological handicap. He'll hold you this once and then it will be back to not now I'm busy sorry later not today. She was his indiscretion, his secret flattery, his pick-me-up when another woman looked through him.

Any minute now he will say 'keep in touch', and she will nod as if it is the done thing to catch up now and then with someone who said 'no, thank you' to every bit of you. Wait, he's saying something, something funny.

Ha ha, he says.

Ha ha, she says.

Of course these are two different laughs, laughed, if one listens carefully, separately. A laugh laughed together is altogether a different laugh, because it is the *same* laugh. That has a definite sound to it, a soul, an echo. It fogs up glass with its breath. That laugh is an animal racing ahead to a jungle you just got to see.

What she'd like to do is to take him up a long flight of stairs, cup his face in her hands, whisper 'don't look' in his ear, and step off the terrace in slow motion. She'd live forever then, as a tic on his face, his sweaty palm, spiked heartbeat, stammer. Every time he tried to sleep, there she'd be on the undersides of his eyes.

Not his fault, she tries to be fair, women have the hots for rats. And she had opted not for the average bad boy on a bike but a man morally ill. Someone who won't even meet her eye. All she has to do is de-special him. Shove him off the sofa in her soul.

She tries to see him through someone else's eyes. There are those who may find him reasonable, his trousers aesthetic and earlobe lickable. To her, his words are understandable only for the language they are spoken in, his clothes too branded, bought squinting into full-length mirrors as anxious salesmen hover with ready flattery. And ears? Come on, everyone has two.

She feels a vague nostalgia. For all those times she had wanted him fiercely, had thought she'd faint from such relentless, non-stop want. The tip of his tongue at the nape of her neck. He loves me, she had convinced herself, even when he said all of nothing to her. He loves me, he loves me... *That's the horrible thing about heads, what we think we know.*

She smiles at a toddler poking at the buckle of her bag, and feels the creases and corners of her own self crackle as she eases into them at last, filling them up. The soles of her feet feel buttered and her skull fits the top of her spine with an audible click; the Hansel and Gretel ends of her finding their way back home.

Love is still magical but in a tasteless way, like unicorn urine. Of course it's the unicorn's horn made of alicorn that stores the stardust, and the bladder itself plays no part in its dazzle. But–think about it–how long can even a mythological character hold its pee? And once you acknowledge this, there are urinary infections and ovarian cysts, a fascinating world of facts in itself but somehow lacking in wonderment.

If nothing else, in a country like this, with a population of so many, replacing a human being can't be a problem, can it? In a sparsely populated country, now, heartbreak would make sense…

Seasoned psychologists might disagree but, according to her, by and large there are two types of madness. First, where the madness is visible to the naked eye, freely on display, all speech out of context and asylum the only option. Second, where the madness is hidden, a well-kept secret between man and mind. In the latter, which she firmly believes is hers–the pretence at sanity, the obsession with keeping the slightest bit of lunacy locked in–means constant research into the 'outside' normal world and how they do things, and to blindly copy. This is further complicated by the pressure to affect a social sort of madness, a window dressing of weird, just a touch of the offbeat. Most of the time she gets away with it, her own cute zany. But there are times she is the only one grinning.

He moves his mouth faster with the words he has no doubt selected for their listenability. 'Skulking around.' He widens his eyes to the east and west. 'It isn't right to anyone.'

She hopes he is done. That he won't suddenly throw her that rehearsed smile of terrible urgency that undid her in the first place. That he wouldn't look her up-down, down-up, eyeballs a blur.

She wants to know if she is winning or losing some race on her way out. Compared to all the women he has shaken off, is she going away quietly? How would he remember her among all of them? Was she the butt, the boobs, the mouth or hair? The clinger, the nag, the wanter of more? She's better than who, who and who? She'd gone to him odourless, un-jewelled, in underclothes sober as tap water. No shampoo, no thong, no heels, no deo, no dye, no Brazilian wax. Just her. Any marks for that?

He raises an eyebrow. Like, ask me something, anything.

If you could be a disease, what would you be? Remember, you want to infect millions, be incurable, take down a continent. Where is a good pestilence when you want one? Black Death? Did I hear you say Black Death? You'd make such a nice Black Death!

Great Britain to his Black Death, she demurely crosses and re-crosses her legs, tucks some hair behind an ear, un-tucks it. Turns her head suddenly to the left, his head follows. Looks like she has something to say, then changes her mind. Is about to smile but doesn't when he starts to return the smile.

Oh darling, she thinks, enjoy your different-touchwood marriage.

How she had wanted to know him because she felt she had always known him! It is time now to admit defeat, lay down arms. What does she know about him? All that hovering around, only to know how much she does not know him, would never know him. He could be anyone. Anyone.

Love is life's comic timing. Perhaps it's important to chase after this one big gilt-wrapped box of true love and sob over its box-in-a-box-in-a-box emptiness in order to enjoy the smaller mundane real-er ups and downs of life which, stacked one on the other, are roughly the same height and weight in the end as Grand Passion.

He pays the bill, tells the waiter, 'Best coffee in the world.'

He is caring that way, knows exits define people. This is what he wants her to remember about him the most, how worldly he is, how cool.

They surge by and by to the café doors. Where they stand awkwardly, arms folded on chests, looking out through the glass, and clear their throats. Ahem and ahem.

Shoving her hands into the back pockets of her jeans she speaks her first full sentence, 'Thank you for seeing me.' She is going to ace it, the business of being an ex.

He smiles in the general direction of her, careful not to make this too personal, to not provoke her into a frenzy of talk-to-mes and what-have-I-dones. Neither does he want an emotional call at midnight on his landline.

'Keep in touch,' he is saying and she is left at last to smile at her own joke, however small.

A TALK

Are we what they call the hi-bye types? Because this is it, I guess. Can't believe you are no one I used to know and doesn't look like we'll bump into each other again. This pebble in my hand...wish I could send it skimming over the pond near your childhood home. Where you played all by yourself because your mother died when you were two and your grandmother was busy in the kitchen.

You spoke to imaginary friends—perhaps you sensed me even then, though I was born ten years after you—and were excited by most things they said in return. You shared your secrets with the pillow, into which you sobbed when your father did not come to school the day you won a prize for topping your class. You soon lost interest in academics but achieved success in what was just a hobby—keeping fit. Your fear of death was there from the beginning and, like most people, you knew you'd die someday. So you ran marathons and swam and joined karate classes and opened a gym of your own. You are thin, yes, but jam-packed with muscles. A wiry body and a ready laugh. Of course, girls flock to your gym and want to meet you out of it. They call you handsome and though you shrug in a cool way, you want to elope with each one of them.

Everything about you became tight-fitting—jeans, wallet, days, nights, your whole solar system. You worked, you played, backpacked through Leh, picked up a guitar and followed G minor.

I was born by then, and living a doll's life. My parents had tried to conceive for years and got me on their third IVF, which mutilated my dad's bank balance and my mother's sense of humour. They overreacted to me from the moment I was made.

I never wore a frock twice. Feeding me and entertaining me was all my mother ever wanted to do. I was watched keenly for any talent, and every picture I sketched and clay monstrosity I sculpted will live on in my mother's showcase forever. That is how she will grow old—before she forgets her bearings and existence, before dementia takes its toll and turns her memories into papier-mâché—staring unblinkingly at all my early arts and crafts.

The first milk tooth I lost is set amidst diamonds in my father's ring, shifted from finger to finger as he swelled over the years. He says the happiness of having me has given him a potbelly all over. Rubies cup my baby canines in marmalade chandeliers mother wears in her ears only on grand occasions.

Remember when you, with a heart beating fast, agreed to meet Sharu's mom alone? That was the first time you touched a woman and you wanted to lick her all over, puppy-like, although you couldn't stop calling her aunty. She was, after all, Sharada's mom, and when you visited her home, aunty made tea for you until the day she rested, deliberately, her foot on yours, and you met her eye in a new way.

You were useless in the back of her SUV, though your body–the body you believe in so implicitly to obey commands and do what you want it to do and be what you want it to be–went away all on its own, surprising you with its mind, will and total lack of morals. It will take you a while to go back to that excitement, after me I mean, but life's little madnesses will get you again...

Verse will approach at night
Urgent, in a mood to fight
You must pretend to give in
To paranormal bits of djinn

How proud you were when you bought your first car, this after having fought so hard with your dad for the scooter he gave you when you grumbled about bus rides being tedious.

'Buy it with your own money,' he had snapped, and fury frizzed your hair.

You got this second-hand Santro two weeks ago. You lived in it, dreamt of it at night and baby-talked to it.

When you met me that first time we did not look at each other. We are a circumspect two, cosy in our own orbits, and perhaps schoolgirls are not eye-catching enough for you. But the second time our eyes did meet. You screeched your car to a halt and glared at me.

I had glared right back, as daddy calls me Shehzadi and I can do no wrong.

Then you made a sound, a disgusted sound, which rarely (rarely!) comes my way, and reversed and drove away. I stared at the back of your car, happy with its dent and dust. You didn't deserve any better, I thought smugly and went my way, never to think of you again until now. Until this minute.

I had finished talking to a friend, come to the road and then charged into the bus stop again to tell her something I'd just remembered. My feet slowly backed into the road and, because my eyes were still on her, I saw my friend's face change from sweetness to slow and sticky panic. It filled her face to the full, this panic, but before the meaning of such dread could communicate itself to me, I began to arc.

I saw my shoes walk the sky. Something warm splashed on my face and turned cold in an instant. A question fluted within, vanished. My fingers were the last thing I felt; they crawled out from under me and clawed at mud. One hand clenched this pebble while the other fluttered once, twice, and then lay down quietly.

Now our hands are touching for the first time. Your hand is red with my blood. A flat and opaque blood, still clumsy from travelling my veins, too surprised to clot. You know, even as you scream, that I am no more, that my breath, my being, my life and laugh are all things of the past. You remember yesterday. You remember making that disgusted face and feel more ashamed of that than this. For this is senseless and will not make sense to you or anybody else for a long while.

My parents will arrive before the police or medical personnel as they live nearby, within walking distance. Before that my friend will reach home shaking, and ring my doorbell with all the suppressed fear I saw on her face, and finish none of her sentences. She will need sleeping pills well into adulthood. But she will also seduce many men with her post-me vulnerability. I am the anecdote of her lifetime, what blows up her eyes, hares off her heartbeat and trembles her alphabets. Two marriages later she will forget me somewhat.

My parents, waiting to have lunch with me, will leave the TV on to come here, dishevelled and disbelieving, almost amused in their utter contempt of such a happening and 100 per cent confident of my immortality, and sit to my left and right and interfere with anybody who wants to move my body. Love will make such a nuisance of them. People who make you suffer from a unique arrogance; they presume they will go before you.

And they will ask me over and over again, 'Why are you lying here on the road, beta?'

My bed at home has roseate ruffles and a Barbie theme my mother saw in a foreign magazine. When the stretcher shifts me they will demand small heart-shaped cushions for my head and ankles. They will say loudly that that is how I sleep, *always*. My mother will ask dad to run home and get the cushions, but he won't be able to take his eyes off my face and from then on, quite simply, their moments of fact and fiction will never coincide. Barred entry into the ambulance along with me, they will shove violently at those around and finally be sedated.

Surrounded by policemen and the family-friend lawyer your father has rushed to the spot, you stand at a distance, still unspeaking, still not guilty, still dazed about the why and where and who of me.

STATUS QUO

A bundle in the middle of the bed. At first, as she withdrew, that was what she saw. The image before the eye. What lay in her line of vision. And that was this: two bodies on a bed. In the next second her memory edited what the eye conveyed: two bodies on *her* bed.

A still life of limbs, a portrait of precise positions, framed forever on her old sheet. Definitely two bodies, that was inarguable. Three feet and a hoist knee. She couldn't believe how quiet it was, this slaughter of her own mouth.

Lila had walked into her home in the middle of the day, using the key with minimum flourish as was her practice and, sensing a dull throb in the back of her head—that could, with adequate resting on a pillow, backtrack from a full-blown migraine—sought her cool bedroom first of all. Then this. The bundle. The middle. The bed.

What she saw had two options: to be an optical illusion and dissolve into nothing—when she peeked next there would be only the bed and no bodies, together or separate, on it; or to be true. And if true, truth had two options: it could be no one she knew, not the man, not the woman; or it could be someone she knew, and knew well.

Without any memory of walking back or sitting, Lila found that she had done both in that order. She looked around. Her home, from the room she sat in to the room she had almost walked into, was in darkness, a dark that contradicted the insane sunshine outside. The tall plant to her left waved its leaves, the curtain heaved over an invisible bosom.

She could of course get up and make tea for herself or play some music. Something soft and slow. But this was less bother, she decided, to just sit here.

A woman—a girl really—appeared at last in the bedroom door, head averted, eyes unseeing in the dimness. Lila, who had occupied the dark long enough to see clearly, watched her pick up a bottle of water from the dining table and take it straight to her mouth, lip to rim.

'Use a glass,' Lila wanted to say but couldn't because her voice would have made it all real, this stranger in her home, in a man's shirt that came to her knee, drinking from a bottle that Lila carried on her morning walks.

The girl then walked to the window and gently parted the curtains about an inch. She stood like that, looking out, for the longest time. A snore floated softly out of the bedroom. The sound seemed to stir the girl. She groped along the wall and switched on a light. Lila cupped her eyes and that movement, of her hand coming up to ward off the sudden glare, caught the girl's attention.

'But...' she said.

Lila lowered her hand, eyes still adjusting to the light. It was her husband's shirt, she recognized that straightaway. But vagabonds can break into your home when no one is there, wear your clothes, eat your food and sleep on your bed. Newspapers were full of this. Fairy tales said so. Goldilocks did it.

'Get out,' said Lila calmly.

'I...'

'Get out.'

The girl thought it over. She could dart back into the bedroom and wake him up. But what could he say, do? In hindsight, both women would come up with a million scenarios, a million ways this could have played out: the confrontation, the matter of victor. But right then the math of the moment was just this command, full of authority and ownership. Get, it said, out.

The girl got out. No fuss, no further attempts at speech. In that long shirt sure to look comical in the cold light of day, from the lift to the pavement, till she flagged down some form of transport and reached an address of her own where she presumably had a cupboard full of clothes her own size.

And Lila watched her go as intensely as she had watched her emerge from the bedroom ten, maybe fifteen, minutes ago.

∽

'It is funny,' said Rinku without a smile, 'to see how people try to hide affairs.'

As usual, the word 'affair' made Lila's bra tighter, as if her body was preparing to do battle, as if the word could rob her of her share of oxygen.

'It's the saddest thing, men in midlife crisis. All that hardcore gymming in track pants and hair an impossible black. I heard,' here Moni's voice dipped ahead of a delicious secret, 'Vijay is seeing some woman.'

The Orphanage for Words

'Oh, poor Parimal,' said Rinku. 'Does she know?'

'Wives know. They know last, but they know.'

'I saw him, I saw him,' panted Tessie. 'They had come to the club together, Vijay and Parimal. Very happy they looked.' She frowned, trying to go back to that time, when husband and wife had walked in and she'd had no idea all was not well between them, damn.

Moni said, 'Running that place has made me clairvoyant.' She owned a spa resort where a lot of couples, more unmarried than married, came on weekend trips.

'A wife, a real wife, just rolls her eyes at the reception, enquires about tea and coffee and room service and freebies. She tries to read what her husband is filling in and corrects him constantly on address, on grammar, on every bloody thing. She smiles to the staff behind his back as if saying, *I married a moron!*

'The girlfriend, on the other hand, is all self-conscious, demure smile, and when the valet comes in, you bet she won't put her hand out for the car key. A small, smart case, hair all done, some nude lipstick going on, and she will never glance once at him. Instead, she will stand very straight, meet no eye, and look closely at the artwork. The paintings, always the paintings. And when we give them the room key, the two will walk politely to the lift and I go awwww, so sweet, all that sex. Like reading the last page in a romance novel.'

'But tell me,' said Rinku earnestly, 'what do the girls get out of this? We know what the men get, but the girls…? They get dumped at some point. The minute they act like a wife, in fact. No man wants two wives! They won't rock the boat, only the rented bed.'

Lila smiled, as did the others. All these stories of other people's infidelity! She fanned herself with the menu and was the first to see Jennifer walk in. Whose eyes were still scrunched against the sun outside with her top lip pushed up to accommodate this scrunching, revealing her upper teeth all in a row. Which suggested, wrongly, mirth.

'Hey!' Lila put the menu down and waved at the approaching woman. Jennifer settled down opposite Lila.

'We were just talking about Vijay and his little girl,' Rinku informed Jennifer.

Here we go again, thought Lila.

Jennifer leaned forward conspiratorially. 'I really gave it to him.'

'To Vijay?' asked Rinku.

Impatiently Jennifer shook her head. 'Not Vijay,' she dismissed, and then paused for dramatic effect before saying, 'Biju.'

Since Biju was Jennifer's own better half the others were torn between curiosity and faking sensitivity.

'What do you mean?' asked someone eventually.

'See,' began Jennifer, obviously having decided earlier on to punish her husband thus by broadcasting his misdemeanours, if any. But the waiter came to take their drink orders and Jennifer squinted at him, demanding to know everything they had to offer by way of beverages, husband forgotten. There was some expected long-winded talk then about certain drinks you could get only in certain places, and by the time they placed their orders and the waiter understood them all clearly they were quite exhausted verbally. Thank God it was a buffet, thought Lila, or this confusion would continue indefinitely.

'You were saying?' someone prompted.

Apparently, despite the fact that Jennifer *never* looked at Biju's mobile phone, that one day, that one time, she did. He had been sleeping when she saw an SMS from some girl way too junior to him at office, saying simply: 'where r u?'

'No "sir", no nothing, and she's fresh out of college,' fumed Jennifer.

'What did you do?'

'I called the number and gave it to her.'

'My God! Someone you don't know!'

'I have met her once.'

'What did she say?'

'Nothing. What can she say? She said the message was meant for someone else and got sent to Biju by m-m-m-mistake. As if!' The mimicked stammer indicated her success at striking terror in the other's heart.

'Remember what I sent day before?' asked Tessie, the official 'forwarder' of the group, flooding their inbox with links and chain mails they deleted on sight. Everyone accorded her a semi-nod. 'This proves nothing though. It is just one of those things. You haven't caught him pants down. If I were you I would have sent a senti message back, something like, "why, do you miss me?" just to trick the woman into replying and giving the game away.'

Jennifer rolled her eyes. 'I thought of that. But if there was nothing going on in the first place, that could set it off, right? She might flirt back. And then things might actually start between them. I, the idiot wife, will play Cupid!'

It is every woman's nightmare, all agreed as they rolled noodles onto their forks, a young ovulating bitch right by their husband's side, sniffing distance. And all of them, the one-man women, nodded their heads.

Lila waved goodbye, kissed cheeks and promised to call everyone home for lunch soon. She felt pleasantly tired. Not that she had eaten much; she couldn't in company. In fact, all that nibbling just meant inconsolable gluttony back home. Joshua found this funny. That when they came back from eating out she'd first and foremost open the fridge.

'Starving?' he'd ask.

'Starving,' she'd say.

Lila stared out of the car. So humid and hot, an armpit day. A small girl with one leg hobbled up to her window and Lila ignored her. Tried to ignore her. She couldn't have lost that leg naturally, she thought. How horrible! To think that someone cut off the leg only to advance her in a career of begging. No anaesthesia, no stitches perhaps. Lila didn't know how it was done but she couldn't imagine a sophisticated surgery, a hospital stay or a whole lot of money spent on the absent limb.

The girl was tapping the car window but looking desultorily around, already having given up on Lila. As the car moved, Lila craned her neck to catch a bent shin falling out from under her skirt—ta da!—with drum rolls. Please God, please, let there be one. But no, all was smooth. The short skirt fell on the single knee in straight unmoving pleats.

Ten years old and walking on one leg asking for alms. Nothing can be more tragic, thought Lila vehemently. *Nothing.*

But she knew, even as a tear flew out her eye, that her pity was spurious, just another sadism. She would have liked to, under other circumstances, gather this unknown grimy girl and hide her from the world. She turned around to take another look, this time as if for a photograph, and felt better instantly at the look of casual cheer on the girl's face as she balanced against a bannered post peeling a banana.

Versatile is what we are. We get used to anything, take in our stride. Evolution depends on it. Earth spins on it. Lila felt even more tired than she'd done a minute ago before seeing the one-legged girl. She longed to be back home, lie in bed beside Joshua, head on his chest, exhaling as he inhaled. The moment when he slipped into sleep and she felt like a balloon in a child's hand.

It would hit her out of the blue. That day. That moment. That girl. Her bandana of curls. The shirt tail cupping her ass. The 'o' of that mouth, promising oblivion. And the knowledges—insidious, hideous, monstrous, multiplying-by-the-minute—that each had about the other. At this point Lila would desperately throw herself into something, anything: a phone call, an email, drive herself to the mall or a movie. Or Joshua would walk in and her heart would stop monkey-climbing the bars of her chest. They would sip tea in the veranda, look at the newspapers, smile at neighbours coming or going.

The silence between them was an old soft T-shirt that's been in the wash too many times. It spoke of understanding, familiarity, a fifteen-year-old marriage. They could sit like this for hours—in restaurants, when all around them chattered passionately to impress whoever they were with; during second shows in movie theatres; on road trips and long journeys; through his colleague's son's funeral—and not feel the need for words.

Some days he'd wake up like a little boy, not allow her to go to work and take her out, just out. And though she could go back to such whims and see them as guilt or remorse, she wouldn't. For that would rewrite everything.

Lila went back to staring at the road. She had told only one person about what happened. And that one time, as she mouthed the memory, she had a feeling she had got it all wrong, that it had never happened, that she'd imagined it after reading some novel, seeing some film.

'And?' her sister had asked.

Lila had shrugged.

'You never asked him? He had no right to bring her to your house! No right!'

Lila shook her head—it was his house too, after all—but her eyes were wary. Had she done the wrong thing? Should she have shouted and thrown a fit that day? Was she doing the wrong thing right now? Was it right to confide in anyone now, so late?

'Of course,' said her sister, 'he would have put it all back on you. Men do that. It would be your fault there's someone else.'

Lila shook her head again, impatient at Joshua's abrupt disappearance into 'men'. 'I didn't feel like saying anything to him. What to say?'

Her sister gave her a funny look. 'You could have walked out.'

Lila's eyes took in the left corner of the room, dead sure at that moment about the inadequacy of the man-woman/husband-wife/person-person laws laid down by the universe. 'Remember,' she said, 'our maid saying her newly married daughter was being beaten up by her husband?'

Her sister did not respond, just watched her.

Lila began to laugh. 'And remember her advice to her daughter? Go hide under the bed when he begins to get angry and don't come out till his anger is over.'

Her sister laughed too and the conversation detoured like most conversations till her nieces arrived from school, their hands gesticulating and their mouths excitedly scurrying over the events of their day. It had been a pleasant afternoon, that afternoon of confiding in her sister what she dared not talk even to herself, watching those words dive into the present without an undertow.

Because when that girl had gone off like that, obeying Lila's command, honest to God Lila had not known what to do. There was now light in the room that had previously been dark. Joshua still slept on soundly. And mostly everything was the way it had been a while before. If she just went on that way too it would all remain that way, wouldn't it? Nobody could come and force her to acknowledge what she didn't want to, what she had already started to forget.

So she went on and he went on and nobody said a thing. She had brittled for a while, when the phone rang or she walked in back from work. When he cleared his throat or shut a magazine. When they were eating and he put down his spoon. She had waited each time, not breathing. And then it passed, just like that. It was as if they had spoken, had it out, as if he had defended, she had accused.

Lila couldn't, just because it suited her, exile actualities. Thus they came to her at the dead of night. A woman she hardly knew. A man she couldn't not know. Two voices; one gruff, one giving in. Hair stroked, knuckles kissed, jokes joked. In the end that's all Lila would've been, a lover's quarrel.

She'd had to reclaim her bed, sleep in it again, not just lie there like a guest. The first time she had lain on it like a baby in the womb, then her limbs unfurled, her hips grew hooks and her head shot out like a turtle's. She took the bed top to toe, then diagonal in an increasingly anticlockwise motion till she was widely travelled in her own bed.

But come morning Lila awoke as always and the night was over once more. It was always about her, the new day, and about nobody else. Twenty minutes at midnight, that's all she had to give up. Subtract that and you still had a lot of hours left in twenty-four.

∽

On Easter they all gathered at the club. His mother needed a walker these days and the stairs were a bother. Lila and Joshua supported her between them and they joined their large family, welcoming not only the rhyme and raucousness of the day but its paraphrasing of their own moods.

Plate balanced on lap, Lila's sister elevated an eyebrow in Joshua's direction, who was far away near the swimming pool, watching a five-year-old nephew splash around. 'I've been thinking. That girl, she must have been more his type and…'

'Nobody is anybody's type,' Lila cut in with enough force to shut her sister up. Then she said evenly, 'If you have known someone since childhood. Still have his note saying I love you. Cut class and failed exams to watch movies with him. Twice miscarried, saw him through a lay-off and that horrible accident…

'What I'm saying is, he knows me. From scratch.'

She paused. 'And marriages can get like that, too comfy. So comfy that one feels one can walk out and back in anytime.'

Her sister got up to get herself some ice-cream cake. Lila crossed her legs, adjusted her sari pleats in reflex action and glanced idly at her mother-in-law smiling and nodding at someone. Nice to see her out and about though she was beginning to lose her memory a bit, the sequence of remembrances. But who is an honest historian? One should be allowed to time-travel one's own anecdotes, rummage and rearrange. Why, she hadn't even recognized this sari Lila wore as one of her own.

Joshua had picked it out of his mother's cupboard just the other day saying to Lila, hey, this will look really good on you. He had tossed it at her and she had deftly caught it right before his mother.

But today when she saw Lila, she said she wanted one just like it, same colour, a muddy, muted pink. When she began to say, 'But this is yours, don't you recognize it?' Joshua had shaken his head at her and she'd said not a word.

PLANS

It is in a Bangalore pub that I first thought of death. I come here every Friday evening to feel hot and happening. When I am drunk enough to slur my speech I feel adequately social, kiss total strangers and exercise what a jealous colleague calls my 'babe' complex. I still remember the first time I decided to sugarcoat myself. A blow-dry, glitter on lips, minor sartorial adjustments and, hello, I was someone else. Someone who walked in alone into pubs and flirted madly with anyone.

There was no need, I had decided, to let the world know how alone and bewildered I felt about everything the rest of the time. I, who devoured articles about more and more women staying single by choice, now just had to believe it.

This permission I granted me to briefly go nuts in dimly lit places made the rest of the week possible. Five evenings I spent circumspectly silent, tongue stung by amiable bee. Then on the sixth day God clapped his hands in me and said, let there be light. I became the type of woman I usually hated. I laughed loud and went all hyper on the dance floor. But then I had to return home, back to me.

Soon I began to feel an oppressive kind of heat even in the merry moments of the pub. Right there, surrounded by a crowd of my own careful making, I would slump over on the inside. I couldn't take it, this knowledge that no one really existed for me. That all this soulmate crap had passed me by. Why must I put up with the dull sameness of my days? Why must I convince the world about a gaiety I had less and less access to? Why? Because there was a kind of dignity in it. There was none in letting my waistline go, cribbing about my job and lack of love.

But then I began to think that departures can be dignified. Nothing messy or tedious. Nothing to freak my parents or neighbours. Just a nice, clean exit. And where would that be? Hanging by a white veil: 'With this ring, I me wed'. Or at a party with a pistol. Bang, sorry about the wall. Or, well, anywhere. Home *is* where you hang yourself.

I smiled into my glass. Drink is known to have this effect and I so did not want my suicide to be a cliché.

'Of course she killed herself, look how neat she left everything. Such a Virgo!'

Or, 'Oh, you know, no husband, no children at her age. So far away from home. What else could she do? Tch, tch...'

I refuse to go in such a mundane way, unleashing a million I-told-you-sos. Mine would be a special death. In my death, as in my pub persona, I wanted attention, to be the life and soul of the party, my own Page 3.

Suddenly life was more interesting. There was something to look forward to. Planning a classy end appealed to the pseudo-intellectual in me. Nothing sustains like the promise of death. In fact, from early adolescence I had the feeling, this *surety* that I would die before thirty. (Really, at twelve, thirty just sounds so dead-body.) To this end, I first grew iffy with food. Gave up meat, then milk, curds, cheese and butter. From thereon it was easy to work on an indigenous digestive salvation. My grandmother, of course, moaned to one and all, 'Nothing this child eats. Nothing.' And this obsession with my eating—as I saw it—repulsed me more. Instead of growing up, I was paring down. My breasts barely breathing in bras too polite to say a thing. I peed once a day, burningly, and menstruated only with a handful of pills.

Soon I was put on a night bus to Bangalore where, it was hoped, I would study engineering and burst forth on the engineering world via engineering inventions for future engineers. Through it all—the godawful childhood years of being an average student with average looks and average social skills—I had grown to hate myself with an unmatched passion. I hated that I had to go through life just like the next person. There seemed to be nothing different or wonderful or meaningful about me and I just could not forgive myself for that.

In my pub life I am so careful not to be the me I hate that I never let pals from this side cross over to the other. The everyday friends hear me grumble about the pay, shops short-changing me, my flat chest and inability to pray. On weekends, on the other hand, I itch all over with excitement. I smoke and drink and swear with such haunting sweet beauty that they all want to take me home and keep me forever.

But the minute I walk out, even before that if the truth be told, I would feel the darkness descend. A kind of congealing in my core. Once someone commented on it and I almost panicked. The truth, like a dirty bra strap, is just over one's shoulder.

'Is anything the matter?' he asked.

'Matter?' I echoed. I am the icing, man, not a cake you cut in the middle. What you dip into carefully with a finger and lick real slow.

I frog-marched him to an impromptu dance floor where I soon found myself slipping this way and that without any effort. By the time I saw the vomit that lent such unique grace to my hips it was too late. My spiky heels were soggy with it and so was the zari hem of my wraparound skirt. This made it rather difficult to cling to the chic act.

'Shit,' said my Einstein salsa partner. 'That's gross.'

No intention of going all small-town now, not act one, scene two. Someone promptly held up his phone like a sword. I am always swallowing nervously in selfies, a poster-girl for goitre.

'What do I do?' I asked, after my drippy dress had made it to FB. Advice came rapidly but senselessly, like peasants relaying what they overheard their masters speak.

A marketing guy touring down South—what he called India's ass—got up. 'I'll see you home.'

'No,' I said. Well, not exactly said but more like screamed, and felt all eyes fix on me. Suddenly it was like my shirt fell off and my skirt unwrapped itself and I was standing there naked like I did when daddy got the jackfruits out. That was when I had been too much me and needed to be punished. I had to peel off all my clothes and sit on the jackfruit. When I was smaller, I would begin to cry and plead for mercy. But as I grew up, I developed the silence.

He was only a farmer, see, and I was going to the city to be an educated girl one day.

'No,' I repeated in a more controlled, laughy sort of way.

I got into a taxi. In keeping with my practical, outside-the-pub existence I had a cab on call to take me home, high as a kite, in the wee hours of the weekend. Most girls have the same godmother as Cinderella; everything comes apart after 12.

The wind clawed at my hair so I stopped sticking my head out the window; now a carsick cabbie and a baby migraine were my lot. How I wished we'd run into some rash driver and die then and there and get it over with, this stupid weekly drive to nowhere from nowhere.

'*Illi stop maadi*,' I told him on autopilot, which is what I always say when the lights of a tall glass building flash up in the dark. Someone had jumped off the building many years ago when it was new. I often imagine him going through all the paperwork and hassle of buying the flat as if he wanted a place to die in. Or maybe the place wasn't what he hoped it would be, a home.

Here was the jazzy flat I shared with no one, not a soul. Most of my pay went into that flat but was it mine? Nope. I tried to think of nothing in particular and began to feel the burden of this dual existence of my own creation. No, really, who was I? The badass rhapsody others called me or the tail-between-my-legs dog I knew myself to be? More to the point, what happened to me when I was neither? No secret pocket to hide in, no straw to slide into. Time hurts me least where I can see it, on my face, in my hair. Its long-nailed claw is deep in my navel.

I opened my front door, the only one on this floor without a doormat saying 'welcome', and met head-on the mirror hung right at the entrance. Who was that? Don't tell me, let me guess.

I closed my eyes. I knew when I looked next I would see nothing there, no one. I was disappearing because I had wished myself away! From the time I can remember I have wanted to die with such intensity and now here I was doing just that, dying. I knew this with great clarity though my limbs, especially my feet, were part-water. I was afraid to look down; the clothes, I knew, would have disappeared again.

I couldn't move but something beneath my chest began to blow like a trumpet, choking me, pressing down on the rest of me, which was growing nano by the second. Bile at the back of my teeth. All windows open—but no jumping, no jumping. This was only the second floor.

I gasped; it was getting difficult to breathe. My knees buckled and I sat down just inside the doorway from where I could see the rest of my home snake out before me.

I tried to be glad for I hated self-pity. No creep of a husband or snotty brats resenting me for having a life of my own. No…nothing. And then I saw it. There in the corner of the corridor that led to my bedroom loomed a dark shadow. It was here. It had followed me home. Daddy's jackfruit.

No time for the tasteful, aesthetic death. I exhaled with difficulty, thinking only one thing, 'I have to outwit it again. I have to fool the jackfruit.' But where would I run to? If it could cross a border and smuggle out of Wynad at midnight, it could follow me everywhere, even into my happily-ever-after death. Then I realized—and it was really a simple matter, after all—one of us has to go.

With a final burst of energy that almost killed me I lunged towards the fruit. I picked it up, disregarding the porcupine thorns that bit poisonously into the soft skin of my palms, and ran up the stairs with it. The fruit, like my chest, began to grow hotter, pricklier and unbearably heavy. Up the steps, my bare feet stumbling over themselves, sour vomit on my heels, as high as I could go. High as the man who died, higher than I had ever gone. All the while the jackfruit fighting back. Even as I swung it off the terrace and heard its dull thud on the ground below I could feel its displeasure, its downright fury.

Sobbing, I collapsed on a step. I cried in confusion and fear for I knew that since I had killed the jackfruit, I no longer had to die.

HAIR

It was a season of ghosts. First, Ammi said the old trunk up in the garage loft contained a corpse. It has that kind of smell, she said. Also, more importantly, wherever she was in the house and whatever she was doing she felt a strong urge to come to the trunk. It was a pull, she insisted, attributing the pull to supernature.

'There is someone taking me there,' she told Afreen khaala, whom we call Afri-ka.

Afri-ka, the only sister who'd been to the US for higher studies, laughed to pooh-pooh Ammi's fears and advertise her own educational exposure. 'That's just a veham,' she said. Veham was a polite way of calling Ammi cuckoo.

Ever since Abba passed away, Ammi had been rather hoping he would appear thus to demonstrate his devotion to her and the family. 'I'm telling you, you'll be sorry,' she said.

Finding no supporters she rounded up the local tailor's son, an adolescent rippling with muscles. He came with a smile full of servitude, and hope for snacks with tea. Warned against sharing her 'feelings', Ammi merely asked him to lug the iron trunk down. With grunts and groans the boy did just that. He stood by the wall, hoping for a glimpse of what lay inside the trunk. It was very heavy, he added.

Yes, yes, Ammi said, dismissing him to the kitchen where Afri-ka would hopefully serve him a cup of tea without cardamom. After her American stint she was inclined to egalitarian bouts. She taught the cook's daughters in the afternoon when Ammi was trying to sleep. Their giggles floated up the window and disturbed her sleep. I am a delicate sleeper, she had said many times, but Afri-ka just shrugged as if to say, that's your problem.

She wouldn't marry either. Ammi had spoken to reputed families of reputed bachelors—sons, brothers, uncles, nephews, business partners, bosses—but she showed insultingly little interest.

It isn't like you are getting younger, Ammi would mutter after each shot was fired and dodged. Afri-ka's salve consisted of some form of flattery the following day. She'd praise a curry or curtain, and Ammi would forget everything and redouble efforts to look for a husband for her.

Now, Ammi stood pale and trembling before her sister in the kitchen. The tailor's son had just departed but Ammi did not sniff the air for cardamom. Instead she sat on the nearest stool to still her shaking knees.

What is it, Afri-ka asked with concern.

Ammi did not reply, so she went to the garage whose sole vehicular occupant was a bicycle with two flat tyres. The iron trunk was on the floor with its lid open. Inside, first and foremost, was a dead rat.

Must have got in during the last airing, she thought. Under the little body were old papers and black-and-white photographs, some clothes. Nothing... Wait a minute.

Afri-ka shuffled stuff on the right side of the trunk, away from the late rodent. The bright red edge of a garment spilled haphazardly.

My wedding sharara, Ammi said from behind.

Afri-ka nodded patiently. She was used to Ammi's operatic approach to life. When all was calm she would break a glass bangle.

Don't you understand? she whispered.

Understand what?

Today is my wedding anniversary.

No amount of rationalizing could puncture Ammi's gut feeling that Abba's ghost had whisked her to explore the ancient trousseau container and discover her wedding outfit on what was after all her wedding anniversary. She would recount the event and point to the tiny hairs on her arms standing up like soldiers enlisted against their will. See, see, she'd say triumphantly. And we saw, saw.

The next ghost to visit was a foreigner. Afri-ka was reading Chinese history. Soon she went on a China trip organized by the institute where she taught. Upon her return, goodness me, said Ammi, nothing was good enough to be called Chinese anymore.

They don't cook or eat this stuff, Afri-ka said patronizingly, pointing to all the painstakingly made noodles and kofta manchurian Ammi had made.

This is Chinese, Ammi said with a dangerous glint in her eye.

No, said her sister, Chinese this is not. They eat more bland and there's soup in their noodles more often than not. Also, she added, what's with the garam masala?

Ammi, whose Chinese food was legend within familial circles, retaliated by not cooking it anymore. There was no boiling of egg noodles or tossing them under cool tap water and mixing them with diced vegetables and the grand finale of mutton keema garnish.

The following Sunday Afri-ka said she knew a Chinese recipe, mind you, word of mouth, and she was going to make it. Ammi feigned unconcern, lolled about before the TV and joined in—louder than necessary—with the canned laughter.

What is this? she asked later when lunch was served, and the only dish to emerge out of Afri-ka's frantic deliberations in the kitchen was a wilted tray of vegetable bits.

'Stir-fry,' she replied. It is full of vitamins.

'So, are these like pills?' Ammi asked to needle her.

'Eat and see.'

The verdict was out: everyone liked the stir-fry except Ammi who pursed her lips. Just vegetables, she dismissed, rinsing her mouth at the washbasin. For her, nothing but meat was real food.

But at the next making of stir-fry, Ammi appeared in the kitchen on some pretext or the other and observed proceedings from the corner of her eye.

Nothing to it, she soon declared. Just vegetables thrown in left and right and then stir stir stir. Anyone can do that, any halfwit, any child, *anyone.*

But when Afri-ka went on an outstation excursion and Ammi stirred the fry, there was a marked difference in taste. Ammi did not mention this to her when she returned but she got to know and asked Ammi, 'Do you want to know how it is made?'

'Me?' asked Ammi with an incredulous laugh. *Me?* And the matter rested there.

Afri-ka's mild fever, which was now a regular occurrence, sometimes gave her migraines. After the cook's girls had gone she went to lie down. In the evening, Ammi said, the poor girl is tired from too much studying, don't wake her up. But at night Ammi crept close and laid a hand on her forehead. The fever was negligible but still it worried her, this relentless plateau of heat, going neither down nor up.

She dabbed her sister's face with ice water and settled for the night right next to her. Sometime after midnight Afri-ka sat up with a loud screech. With a thudding heart Ammi listened to her babble...in pure Chinese!

Bas, Ammi had the diagnosis ready next morning. It is a Chinese invasion, she said, of Afri-ka's soul. A spirit had possessed her when she was in that country and now Allah help her. When Afri-ka laughed, she pointed at her crinkled eyes. Look, Chinaman eyes. It was true that Afri-ka's eyes had changed colour. Ammi was all for calling the maulvis but Afri-ka said it was just the fever.

Ammi had to wait till she slept, to practise her witchcraft. The cook's wife, in lieu of tuition fees, brought in the exorcist, though he called himself a doctor for the dead. He circled—very cautiously—Afri-ka's bed and handed Ammi a taveez to be tied around her arm. That was a big challenge, getting Afri-ka to even consider looking at the charm. Finally, to get rid of Ammi, she wore it hidden under her long kurta sleeve.

But the fever did not go and Ammi began to worry that the slit-eyed ghost still sat within her. When Afri-ka suggested stir-fry again Ammi almost jumped out of her skin. That's not our food, okay? You get well and then we will think about making it.

Afri-ka pretended to pull her hair out in frustration. Don't do that, Ammi said promptly. You are losing all your hair as it is.

And that was the third and final ghost to flit in that summer. Hair. Afri-ka lost all her hair in chemo. She grew thin, too, and looked exhausted all the time. But the baldness was the real shock. Earlier Ammi used to comb her hair very, very gently, trying to retain what there was.

Let's get you a wig, she said, in a jolly way. But Afri-ka said no, I don't want a wig. She had seen people with lopsided hairpieces and did not want to have that. Or an itchy scalp.

But then she began to see her hair everywhere. In the food. In the kitchen drain. In the basin, on the road, in the doctor's mouth, everywhere. Look, she'd point to Ammi, look, there's my hair.

Poor Ammi. She'd hurriedly make some explanation to the other person. My sister is not well, she'd mumble shamefaced. The illness was taking its toll on her too, on all her plans to lock her sister into blissful matrimony. And this madness…she was afraid, would be the last nail.

But in the night she'd stroke her sister's head, kiss it and whisper, it is here. All your hair is here. I can see it.

FATHERS

He is a self-made man. A strong, active, rational person who lives for others. This is true except for the tense; the 'is' is now 'was'. After ten wordless days on a ventilator following a massive stroke, he left an early a.m. in September.

My brother and I often escaped to the hospital canteen for tea. 'Too sweet,' we kept saying, not once mentioning the ICU. When docs suggested brain surgery or dialysis we would start off by saying 'no' and end up nodding, for the alternative of losing him right away was unthinkable. The idea was to keep him going despite the laboured breathing and resolutely shut eyes.

The first time we saw him like that was not easy. We put our hand in his. Squeeze my hand if you are in pain, I said, and he didn't squeeze my hand. It didn't matter what the doctors thought—they were bound to be cynical. We shooed away a priest; 'If he sees you, he will think he is dying or something.'

A minute in the morning, a minute in the evening was all we got with him. Two minutes in twenty-four hours. And we could go in only one at a time. If I saw him one morning, then my brother saw him that evening and mother, the next morning, I saw him only next evening. Sixty seconds to get him to show some sign he was still with us. 'He moved his foot,' I would say, 'he moved his toe.' But in the hospital records, this patient never tossed, never turned.

It rained continuously those days so that visitors landed up drenched and frowning. Most felt we should go in for a second opinion, shift him to another hospital, take him abroad. They thought we were doing nothing. And there were those who thought that a good thing, that we were doing nothing. He's had his life, they said in a consoling way.

My brother and I strategized the daily monologue for his bedside, knowing he would be worried over where he was, what was happening to him, Mom's state of mind...I'd joke, hoping he was laughing inside, and then I'd sing into his right, working ear a song he loved. This was tough as his favourite songs were old Malayalam ones with lyrics we had to Google. In the hushed atmosphere of the ICU, surrounded by the semi-conscious or comatose, to sing badly a song you've never sung before, hoping your dad is listening...at the time seemed the most natural thing to do.

We blinked stupidly when told he had just another five minutes left. He was the most fighting-fit seventy-nine-year-old ex-military man we knew. *Five?* We stared at him blankly, sure we could reach him if only we knew how.

The man who showed us the same movie twice so we could study the extras or a junior artiste. Had a barber come home first Sunday every month to give us, son and daughter alike, a crew cut. Long hair, jewellery, talcum, kohl, posh clothes—he had declared war on these. As a family, we were vain about not being vain.

Then he came off the ventilator. Dad was demoted to dead and there was not a thing we could do about it.

A funeral manager whisked him off for a shave and a bath. The hour we waited for dad to be spruced up was spent back at the canteen over tea, thinking about what a doctor had said. That the day he was brought in, dad had pleaded not to be hooked on to any machine that would prolong his life artificially. That's him, we said unemotionally. That sounds just like him.

I travelled with dad in the ambulance. We both maintained silence, a deeply offended one on my part. I was thinking about my funeral phobia; I had managed to evade every bloody funeral until then: my best friend at the age of five, three grandparents, an aunt, and sundry acquaintances and neighbours…none had me condoling live at the burial. Also, all the ones I *had* seen were in Bollywood films where pristine white covers the corpse and the bereaved, a hummable song plays and a little pot is tipped delicately into the Ganges. Most of all, one knew the dear departed would get up to die in another film. So this was my first funeral.

The mobile mortuary kept dad fresh in our drawing room, ready to greet guests. Nuns placed roses on his chest and head. Since the funeral was next noon, the whole night was spent praying by his side. The front door was open (it can be locked only after the funeral) and no tea was boiled at home. Neighbours pitched in seamlessly, used to the rhythm of departures. I could see what dad meant when he'd once explained why he wouldn't move out to live with me in another city, or with my brother in another country:

'I am too old to set up home elsewhere, and begin this lovely circle of friendships again. It takes a lifetime.'

From the moment he froze on his chair that fateful morning to the last splash of earth on his coffin, there was no dearth of those who were there for him.

After the seventh-day service in the church, we slept. For two days straight we slumbered as if drugged. And woke to the implacable hard fact of his disappearance. We can't see his death as anything less than wilful desertion.

All his shirts are hanging in his cupboard. His aftershave still hits our nose when we open the bathroom cabinet. His toothbrush, his glasses, the book he was reading, his medicines, everything is exactly where he left them. His blown-up pictures are all over our home courtesy kind relatives, his stamp-size photo in a newspaper with his birth and death dates under it.

I know how life works. I understand why a man almost eighty can drop dead. But I also need to know how he is, where he is. And tell him all about the funeral: who came, what they wore, how they ate, what they said about him. Because I tell him everything.

THE CRY

Years of hoping against hope had caught up with her. She stopped timing her ovulation and, in the main, seemed to be accepting a childless fate. She no longer inflicted tests or that high keening cry on her husband, and appeared to give up as he had been telling her to all along.

'Sophie,' he had said many times during their decade of desperate dreaming, 'be sensible.' And it was as if she opted for sense with a vengeance. 'We have no children,' she took to confiding casually in strangers on trains or flights, more, he knew, out of a compelling need to believe it herself and forfeit the urge for miracles.

'Children none,' Sophie declared with a regal tilt to the head, as if entering a land for the barren. A password not for her own arrival anywhere but to point out exits for whoever may find it embarrassing or offensive that here was she, infertile, non-incubating, hatching nothing and no one in nine months from now.

No children, she said in a careful little voice. Without inflection, vowels abrupt, so that it sounded, before the ear may decode all of it, like a word of foreign origin. 'Nchlrn-

nchlrn' to anyone who'd listen, before they even asked, for she wanted it out of the way, the matter of offspring, their age, school and gender.

When someone offered a puppy on her birthday she said briskly, 'No, thank you,' patting the pup as if to behead it. And the guest had no choice but to hold on to his gift, who had vacated its bow-tied straw basket early on, even while eating cake.

Which was a far cry from her staring at a sunlit spot in their home for hours, saying as evening fell, 'It was kind of lavender.'

Truth to tell, they felt lethargic. That, and the memory of the 'honeymoon baby' they almost had in the first year of their marriage, about whom they'd said with careless vanity: 'too early, so unplanned' etc. The one who got away because of an imperfect heart the doctors had detected soon enough with such sophisticated weaponry. They had twisted and turned, asking, asking, but all agreed on the need to abort. 'There will be other babies,' was what they said. And Sophie had asked him, her husband: 'Yes, there will be others, but what about this one?'

She had stayed overnight in the hospital, worn a regulation back-open gown, and plucked at the labour-inducing drip on her arm. The nurses asked her, quite kindly, if she wanted to see it, hold it, the baby with a heart that wouldn't beat. And though Sophie had felt a fluttery brush on her inner thigh—a finger? a palm?—she refused to turn sentimental over the baby who did not make her a mother. She shook her head and the nurses went away with what should have been the apple of her eye.

Then it had begun, the copulation by clock and calendar, the long vigil, the medical onslaught, two feet propped up on a pillow all night, novenas in an out-of-the-way church, non-stop advice from well-wishers, the growing hush deep within her body. Marching in missionary position in the battlefield of their bed month after month, night after night, for ten long years, left-right-left.

'Why don't you adopt?' Sophie's mother asked just recently on Skype.

Susheel had looked at Sophie, too, to gauge her reaction. But with her new no-nonsense air, she said, 'Mommy, give us time to catch our breath.'

It had been traumatic, he silently agreed, but more for her than him. He watched her warily a while for any covert hysteria, but all minor forms of fishwifery were explicable from here on.

And, she added to him in a tone approaching cheer, there is enough time; they were only thirty-five years old. She began to make travel plans, to forward elaborate maps, charts and flight schedules to him, to call up people they knew and ask them, liltingly, about the weather in a certain place and suitable clothes. That summer they were going away—just the two of them—to some secret destination, and discover what they were when just by themselves, without this constant hum in the ear, this expectation of another.

To that end came her general cry of 'we have no kids!' like an unseen amputation or something shot point-blank in air. It was the deliberate manufacturing of another mood.

It was around then that the pregnancy took them unawares. There were no warning signs. The absence of her periods they'd attributed to the regular hormonal injections she used to take earlier to boost her fertility. Her nausea was something she ate—'the prawns,' she grumbled, retching into the bathroom basin—and the pale anaemic air they put down to the clammy weather and her general weakness.

It was only in her fourth month that a routine blood test drove them clean out of their minds.

He had come home clutching the report, his face inscrutable. She took one look at him and sensed doom. 'I am dying,' she thought. 'I am dying and he doesn't know how to tell me. I have damaged myself beyond repair with my invasions of my own body. One should never want what one cannot have,' she was thinking when he handed her the report.

The word danced before her eyes. *Positive.* Positive what? Then she scanned the word overleaf: pregnancy. She sat with a painful thud on the dining table chair, the flat dark wood jarring the base of her spine.

From then on the two of them did everything in their power to drive each other, if possible, madder. Sleep, he'd order, when she wanted to eat nei-roast dosa made in an unhygienic roadside handcart. Walk, he'd nudge her, when sleep smote her down senseless. Most of all she wanted sugarcane juice; to smell, drink, take a shower. And he brought her buckets of it till her blood sugar shot through the roof with gestational diabetes.

The foetal heartbeat rhymed with all those beeping machines; still they ran around, headless chicks, for more tests. 'No, no,' they were shooed off. 'Everything is fine. Nothing to worry.'

Sophie and Susheel rarely let the other finish a sentence for fear of it lapsing into... Instead, they kept in the limelight his clients, the day's headlines, her bowel movement. Non-aligned words, at room temperature. Any reference to due date was reluctant, of the necessary kind, after a scan or when nightmares split the back of her head. Silence was tacit and a talisman. Sometimes he pressed his lips urgently to the nape of her neck and she understood.

Accomplices, they kept the 'good news' to themselves. No point telling her mother or his sister, who would all just worry incessantly, phone constantly or arrive instantly. Off they'd go, loved ones, bumpity-bumpity-bump some staircase, dragging him and especially her with them. No, when it came to stark raving mad they were doing fine on their own. The floppy state of the bedroom, the chaos in the kitchen, the sheer nervous fizz making soda of their blood were proof enough of their own mental displacement.

She began to hyperventilate. This is God's child, she said. Nothing else, she felt, could explain this magic. At another time, forgetting about angels flapping about her room with celestial messages, she'd proclaim it the devil's own sperm.

'Take it out or it will kill me,' she yelled at midnight, louder and louder until mildly sedated. 'I am having triplets or at least twins!' She snatched his hand and put it on her belly. 'Now you can hear them breathe, can't you?'

Oh, go to sleep, he said.

He couldn't pamper her every day. His job—he was a lawyer—was complication enough, and he should not take too seriously what his inner voice whispered were merely 'feminine' fears. He had to conserve his strength for later. One had to get through this, the interminable dullness of the waiting room. He hoped to hell the third trimester would end earlier than indicated. His friend's wife, who was Sophie's obstetrician, had winked the last time they met: 'Pick out an auspicious moment, choose any star, avittam or thiruvadira, and we'll take the baby out that day.' Apparently, horoscopes were negotiable.

Sobbing piteously one Sunday after Mass, Sophie told him her mind was tricking her into wanting 'only bad things' for the baby. 'Make my mind go blank,' she pleaded. 'How can I want my baby to be anything but perfect? I throw him down cliffs and put him under the wheels of a truck. I am a bad mother. I can't be mother at all…'

She knew, 100 per cent, that when the time came and they cut her open, they'd find:

a) nothing
b) a monster with two horns, a tail
c) a stuffed toy
d) a foetus dunked face-down in its own amniotic fluid

Option D, click-clicked a tongue in her head, option D. Insomnia was her ally against sanity, and Susheel said many things in many tenors to her—from sweet nothings to fuck-off—that made sense only as and when being said.

The surety that enemies were plotting against her tied her stomach up in knots. The doctors were lying, there was no baby, and if there was one it had no head, no heart.

Her own physical misshapenness, that all called fleeting, was taking its toll. She caught her bump in mirrors, in shop windows, but never looked at it directly if she could help it. Didn't want to *see* what was inside her, speckled, the colour of espresso, with a gooey centre. And self-detonate.

She took to flushing the folic acid, the calcium pills, vitamin this, vitamin that, down the toilet. Who knew what was in them? Whom could she trust? Whom could she turn to? Best, she decided in a moment of fatigue, to pretend faith in her husband, for there were long intervals when he seemed to her the villain of the piece.

∽

When the time came and her salwar was drenched, they, without a fuss, drove to the hospital in a flash. Above all, they did not want to hope, or at least let on to each other that they were hoping such hopes where all hopes led to one hope:

just live, make it out of there into here please.

As the labour intensified, he sat down next to her and the two of them said nothing, not a thing, their mouths dry, ears clogged.

'One baby coming up!' said the doctor merrily.

A muted huh huh huh wisped out of nowhere, soft, offended.

'A boy,' said someone to someone else. Then silence.

Sophie lay back, convinced that nothing was right. She watched with droopy eyes a nurse walk over to Susheel and hand him…

'What is it?' she asked with a return of panic.

He shook his head and bent over her, to place in her arms. She trembled once violently, as if to stop him. Wary and numb she looked down then with the slowest of eyes.

A microscopic nose, tangled lashes, skin too loose to fit yet. She breathed out in a whoosh, though she knew it was rash to think everything fine. She was yet to meet his eyes, count his toes, feel the pulse in that diaphanous wrist.

She would have thrown her head back and laughed loudly—for she knew instinctively that she would have wanted to laugh at this point—but could feel neither her head nor neck or, for that matter, was unsure of working up a smile, let alone a laugh. Her very skin seemed to be turning inside out this minute, ripping inarticulately from the back of her to the front.

In the last eleven years Sophie had rehearsed many words with which to welcome a child of hers into the world, but as of now, to be honest, all of language was a sob in her chest. She thought, lucidly enough, 'But I don't even know you,' and burst into tears.

A MAN

At the back of my mind are always the census people. They who come at an unspecified time in the morning or afternoon with little white forms that need filling. To these official record keepers of the nation I confide my deepest pride and achievement: Married (tick). I offer them water and tea, in that order, and smile like I did in my wedding snaps–hiding my slanted tooth with a trick of the lip. Unmarried is the other option, for divorcees, widows, lesbians and all those new women who call themselves bachelors.

In the 'No. of Children' section I draw a blank. Nil, they write, their spectacles gleaming in the natural light of my dining room where I seat them for the availability of a table to write on. I wonder if they have a column on babies that almost got made, for kids one almost had or may have in the future. Because if that counts then I did carry one quarter term. But they don't ask, I don't say. They are interested in hard facts, the here and now, how many, in what they can see, count on their fingers and make a note of. Brilliant at math they are, with pet names for every number.

I remember being asked many times, even before I married. With girlfriends in ice-cream parlours, with grandparents at funerals, in trains and buses by total strangers: how many children will you have? As if the uterus is you, as if you only have to say a magic number and, bam, the babies are there, grinning in quick succession.

They take down the age too—my husband's and mine. There is a gap of two years between us. This keeps me the younger of the two, respectful and apologetic. I am by default the compromising one, the adjuster, the suck-up.

The census-takers nod. I only have to open my mouth and they nod. But I keep their nods in mind as I open my mouth so that it is a non-vicious cycle of words and nods.

I've always had difficulty with comments like the little cunt or such a prick or an asshole, not from prudery but a hesitation to imagine whole people walking the earth independently as genitals. Or 'she is such a pain', 'he eats like a horse'…dismissing or exaggerating what are only human beings. No, I prefer this neat numbering of people down to one, two, three, not taking into account joint pains or phobias. Everyone is every one in the census forms, like in the eyes of God. I like that.

I sign here and here and they go next door where Mrs Sharma will offer them water, tea and the numerable facts of her life.

After they leave, I invariably think of what didn't go into that form. A basin glutted with hair—every time I comb they descend in mobs. How I never eat noodles in polite company. My belief in ghosts that leads me now and then to stand before a mirror in the dark with a candle, whispering names of dead people I used to know…

Stuff nobody wants to know. Statistics are what they are after and then they say thank you and run, just about remembering to meet my eye at the door.

This man I loved long ago, foolishly and smugly, was much older. I was a student, his student, a sitting duck. I was flattered and fluttery and little girl and all his. He was such a stern man that one never thought of arguing, not even with his offer of affection. His wife was also a professor and worked in another college, another city. He was always 'helping' me with my course and the sex was mostly in broad daylight in his room with the door slightly ajar. This kept me compliant but not as participatory as I would have liked. But whenever he suggested a hotel room for the night, I hesitated. Here in his room I could pretend it was spontaneous, and on full-moon nights turn into a howling creature, howling for him.

I was a word whore, storing up everything he said. His thoughts on any subject under the sun I sought with such ferocity, memorized and quoted. Creeping out of my room with reference books and ready-made excuses was exciting. It was the age difference and the fact that he had never come on to a single student before me that protected us. By the time the scandal that rocked the nation about another professor and student broke out, we were done. I had missed a period and he'd had his scare. Plus, he never said a word against his wife, not even at the peak of our affair. There was no question of anything but the present tense.

'My wife loves me too much.'

He could say that and still be the man who broke my heart for the three long years it took me to graduate and for hearts to break. And he could say it with the sympathy and satire such sentences required to be said. He got me a sun made of wood from one of his holidays abroad. A wooden sun with wooden rays, the rays raying into the wood of the cupboard I hung it on so no sun fell on his sun.

Those days I was in between two versions of myself. Not queen, not washerwoman. Not stinking rich, not fragrantly poor. Spineless, smiling, head in a nod, I was, like I am now, the one who copes with one's lot. But to be fair to him, my chest turned 38 when I was thirteen.

Whenever I think of that episode in my life, I rush to catch my reflection in the mirror, car window, any shiny surface. I don't know—I think I wonder about how I feel now about then. I had once heard of a colleague's husband having cancer. When he dropped in at the office, I had run breathlessly down the stairs five floors just to catch a glimpse of him. To see I don't know what.

These days I hardly think of kissing. In fact, after the third filling I barely even laugh for fear of exposing the ugly black bits. But back then I lived to kiss. Having been to the main act and back, he was hardly going to swoon because our lips met, but if he had let me just kiss him and kiss him I think we would still be in some dark corner, kissing.

When my husband hurries through his breakfast—what I cook after waking up earlier than him with the aid of an alarm clock—or snaps at me irritated, or unpins my hair at half past eight, I compare him in an easy uncalculating manner to him, my first love. 'I feel so guilty when thoughts of other men come to my head,' I told him just the other night.

'My dear girl, heads are for thoughts of other men,' he laughed. And I shivered because either one of them could have said that. Maybe we pick our men for their similarities. We are what we are, the 'I' in us wanting the opposite of us, which makes composites of all those we love.

Kiss to climax my husband is mute, while the other used to say raw things, mmmm things, things in his mother tongue. Now I am the jabberer, the one who chats up a storm before, during and after, while those days I just lay there with index finger on lips, tongue banished to the back of my throat.

Love. This word I reserve for the professor, the one who tutored my heart, the king of the kingdom of me. My husband was a decision, an instance of sanity and sense. Not a single goosebump shot up my arm, no physical callisthenic taken out of context and crying my eyes out. He is hot and not hot. I don't look at him across a room and die to rip his clothes off. We lie on the same bed, he and I, side by side every night, my head on my pillow, his head on his pillow. No 'tell me what you're thinking', no quoting from collections of poems.

When he makes a move it is nice. And even if I don't feel a thing up until the end it is enough to be wanted. To want… now that is another story. And women have this down to an art; a man in hand, another on mind and somehow we know how and when exactly to bring them down to one in number. Reboot in Safe Mode.

You see it in birds, this sudden decision. Ardour, passion, crazy, mad for each other head-over-heels-ness. Two birds are flying one way, so perfectly in sync. Two left wings, up, two left wings down. Two right wings up, and so on. Then, en route, enter the third bird at a tangent and one of the pair detours and dips in a perfect arch with this new bird. Everyone is special, one at a time. You see it in birds, unmarried birds.

It came as a mild shock and yet no shock at all when I bumped into—while foraging for submissive ladies' fingers—an old classmate who spoke about *him*. 'Are you in touch with him?' I asked casually, my eye firmly on the vegetable in my hand, when we were done with 'imagine meeting you here' and 'you look the same' in a high pitch.

'He has lost it completely.'

My eyes jumped to hers. 'What do you mean?' Whatever did she mean? My heart began to beat loud and lurid.

'He is not well,' she said meaningfully.

'Is he dying?'

'I wish!' She laughed as we walked down the mall aisle. Girls in heavy make-up squirted free perfume on our wrists.

We edged into a café by the side. 'It is not hot,' she complained to the waiter about her coffee. I waited patiently for her to win the war and return her attention to him, the man I used to love so desperately.

'It is his mind,' she said at last. 'He is just not…there. And his poor wife! All their savings gone in treatments, she had to move into a rented house. Apparently his father had Alzheimer's too, so it is not really a surprise. And all these brainy types are the first to go.'

'Can you,' I asked her impulsively, 'get me his address or phone number? I would like to…visit.'

'You will go all the way to Pune?'

'Maybe I'll call,' I said vaguely.

I think my heart safe now. No trusting no lusting no licking ass. If a crocodile wants to eat it, my heart hangs high on a tree where no one can reach.

This journey is silly, I told myself over and over. It is self-indulgent, foolish and sentimental. It has no place in the scheme of things. It interferes with reality, with the forward motion of life. Throughout the journey—I intended to arrive unannounced—I flashbacked compulsively. Not only did I get it wrong, but I planned plans, dreamt dreams, fantasized fantasies based on how wrong I got it. For instance, the coolness in his eye now and then that I took to be traditional manly disdain for female nonsense. Or the time when I couldn't make it and he said something cutting to me in class in front of everyone and I'd smiled.

His remark and my conditioned response were not important then, only that I had no choice about the congealing that had begun deep inside me. The surety when replaced by hesitation, my feet were the first to protest. I would sit as if glued to the chair or bench or cinema seat even while my eyes would seek out the clock and fix there in an agony of knowing that I would not, in the end, get up to go and meet him on time, that I couldn't even stand up to make a phone call from a public booth to inform him of my not coming.

At the time I had taken my cue from him. The removal of a not-yet-here foetus, he implied, was not important enough to halt us in any way. And I copied his nonchalance, looking up as I did to him in every way. Also, it was difficult to talk anyway about things your body and mind could not grasp or hold on to. I was then all of nineteen and he forty-six.

That first day in class I had not known a thing. Just stood there trembling. The ugly duckling now grown into an ugly duck. I was homesick and insecure amidst so many confident classmates. They all spoke English so well and dressed differently from me. All my salwar-kameezes, stitched by my mother with her own two hands, hung on me like a poor man's washing. He said he had noticed me, that I had caught his eye, that I was going to be someone. The last I think I thought, he probably never said that; the heart lives hand to mouth.

'Come over,' he had said casually to me in class. When I went, he spoke of everything but me till I wept into pillows.

'I love you, sir,' I said at last, when I could take no more. And he spoke of something totally removed. When I left that day he patted my back as if I were a child. Maybe he sought to step back, do the right thing.

It was I who couldn't let go. Me, brought up by a widowed mother who thought the slightest tenderness would spoil me, make me unfit to live in a world where tragedies were the norm. Who saw to it that my pulse, my heartbeat, not a leaf in me stirred. But in a land of no songs, someone is bound to hum. So I was back with more passionate declarations of love, they just flowed out of my mouth with a mind of their own, these words. Love. I. You.

I began to talk and sit and dress provocatively, as provocatively as my homemade apparel, small-town upbringing allowed. And he pretended not to notice this growing fever within me. Which of course unhinged me to the point of rabid, like someone was turning my volume knob higher and higher. Until one day without rhyme or reason I shouted right into his mouth–by kissing him.

I was a thanker. Grateful and gushing. Wanting only to display good manners and good breeding and brushed

The Orphanage for Words   61

teeth all in a row. My spine bowed willingly, suppliantly and the smile was all the more sweet for having nothing to say.

I remembered now without rancour, my eye prickled by the dry agricultural lands stretching outside. In the end the love I swore died. I stopped soulmating. I hated him, his smile, his way of tilting sentences upwards as if towards a question mark, his touch. It was like someone I did not know had been living in my vagina and had now walked out.

The train took me to his hometown in twenty-four hours flat as promised. I was going to be there for half a day, then I'd board a return train. My plan was plain: meet him and ta-ta. I was doing it out of respect and nostalgia and a misplaced sense of guilt.

Finding the house took me lesser time than I thought, and sooner than I expected I was tentatively unlatching a rusted gate in a crowded locality. A stray dog whimpered at my arrival and watched my progress from gate to door with pus-filled eyes and an imperceptible wag of tail. The doorbell startled the dog and me.

No one came to the door though I could hear faint noises inside. A swish and a swash. Some pot wobbling on a metal surface. I pushed the door a little and it opened.

'Who?' called out a voice, his wife's. She looked at me without surprise. 'Student?'

I nodded.

'I am sorry I don't remember you,' she said.

'No, no,' I said, finding my voice. 'We never met.'

She left me standing there and went back inside the room. I stood there heavy and faintly reeking of sweat. All my bulk came at me with a vengeance. I felt dizzy then and parked myself gingerly on a worn-looking sofa. She was back in minutes, wiping her hand on her sari pallu. 'It is sad,' she said without any sadness, as if to kick-start my own flow of platitudes about her situation.

'You used to teach too...' I said.

She said yes, yes impatiently as if I was talking about someone else. 'Will you have some tea?'

'No, no,' I said, equally polite. 'I heard about sir and I just had to come and see...'

'It is okay now,' she said. Then she brightened up as if expecting some minor miracle from me. 'Some of his students did a collection for him. That paid half of his hospital bills...' Her voice trailed off.

'I was his student fifteen years ago.'

She nodded without interest. I realized that he must have had a million students through his teaching career, that to her I must look like an example of those faceless throngs he sought to educate once upon a time. Maybe she saw each student as a personal enemy, who had kept him from her all through his youth and lucidity.

'Is there anything I can do?' I asked on impulse.

'Nothing...' she shook her head. 'I have to cook now. These sedatives make him very hungry... Oh, you can get me some vegetables from just around the corner. Or you can sit here with him while I go and come back. Yes, that's better. You sit here and I will just pop out for a second.' Her eyes were bright now, at odds with her earlier manner and the dull sari she wore.

'Of course,' I murmured in mild alarm. 'No problem.'

'Just sit here. He is sleeping. Drugged sleep, won't wake up anytime now. Still, I never leave him alone.'

She picked up her chappals and threw them out the front door one by one, then she crossed the threshold and slipped her feet into them. Briskly she set off to the gate, past the dozing dog.

I sat there frozen, grappling with geography, with where I was, the place, this spot. It reminded me of all the times I had sat towards the end of our association trying to get up and go and meet him. 'Hippy,' he used to call me. 'You are such a hippy.' Not because I was in any sense of the word anything of the sort, but simply because it occurred to him to call me by a nickname, to accord me some status, to evoke whatever hippiness was in me, I suppose, to suit his own purpose.

Each step I took was hard work, to place feet one after the other in his direction. And there he was, my former teacher and boyfriend, lying with his back to me. Under the thin white kurta I could make out his vertebrae. I hovered a little inside the room, fascinated by the fan on the ceiling, the two back-to-back books on the table, the bottle of water by his side.

In the adjoining bathroom I opened the tap, letting the water flow over my wrists, my pulse. I heard him turn over in the bed. Scared now, I returned. He was lying on his back, staring vacantly around. His gaze took me in and I looked back almost audibly. What a racket I was making with my own breathing!

Oh, I had forgotten to shut the tap. Water flowed into the basin with a petulant hiss. I came back to him and saw the damp patch on the sheet under him. What was I to do? Change him? I was averse to touching him, actually touching him, in any way. He licked his lips and looked at me. Those eyes. Colonizing. Uprooting. Pointing out crystal clear A to Z all my inadequacies and every ignorance.

I put out a tentative hand to his face. My hand stayed suspended over his forehead then descended slowly and ended with a fingertip brushing the corner of his eyebrow. It felt no different from touching the picture of an eyebrow. I subsided then, fazed a little by the total forgetfulness on his face. His eyes were wary, suspicious, alert against me. They darted from my hand to my eyes. As he lay back so still, he appeared entirely restless, panicked by my appearance.

With relief I heard his wife come in through the door, the slap-slap of her two chappals being thrown by hand on the floor, the thwack of a plastic packet hitting the kitchen counter. And then she was there with polite gratitude, very sure deep in her heart that she hadn't asked too much of me.

I smiled insincerely, said it was no trouble at all and she grew a little garrulous. 'He doesn't sleep without medicine. Finally the doctor prescribed sedatives for him *for me*! So I could get some rest.' She watched me carefully, if I had gotten that point right, about her lack of rest. Then she noticed that her husband had wet himself. She clicked her tongue. '*Oooof!*' she rolled her eyes as if at a naughty child. I looked away as she expertly, with a hand under his armpit, hauled him up. 'Chalo bathroom,' she said.

'I will be off then,' I said and she nodded absent-mindedly.

'Sonu hungry,' he announced suddenly loud and clear. His voice no different from the way it spoke in class or in bed long ago–full of authority and clairvoyance. As a lover he had been sulky, getting his due with inattention. I almost went to him then, automatically.

'I am yet to start cooking,' she told him with no particular inflection. 'There is bread if you want.'

'Bread,' he said in a jovial way, allowing her to drag him towards the loo. There he paused and pointed at me. 'Kiss Sonu,' he complained, his lower lip jutting. 'She kiss Sonu.'

Explanations and excuses as if by habit flew to my mouth, danced on my tongue. I was ready to self-defend, to extricate myself. But his wife threw me an apologetic smile and shrugged, implying he was babbling, not to be taken seriously. And I complied with her implication.

I complied all the way back home and for two months or so after that meeting. Then I allowed myself to think– perhaps fancifully and with more vanity than anything else–that believe it or not, however improbable, even with the passage of time and his memories in a mish-mash, he had not forgotten. He recognized me, recalled the kiss I initiated in a moment of boot-stomping heartbeats and 100 per cent honesty so long ago. And this is the apportioning of blame his brain has reserved for me: I'm the culprit, the one who started it all, omnipotent, irresistible, tempting little minx me.

At odd times–like before waking up, or mid-surrender to my husband at night, or having a cup of tea before he gets up–this is what I think without thinking, that he remembers.

KITE

Nothing in her eyes no hello no happy birthday. You want the person who gave birth to you to remember the date don't you.

Why do they come here and lecture me on what to do. I am doing the best I can. I just need time. It's all changed, she has changed. She doesn't remember me she doesn't know me and please forgive me I don't know her.

Yes I am going on she is going on we all go on. I get up cook feed her and leave for work keeping the key with a neighbour and come at noon to feed her again before running back to work where that man and his team make me feel like an idiot and I'm back now to feed and bathe her and then what tell me this then what. Am I to go on like this as long as she does? I'm not carrying her with me you know she is taking me somewhere with her I don't know where and do I want to know.

I can't sleep it is past two she is sound asleep with the pills I can hear her snore maybe I should take a pill myself and oversleep and never get up.

Death comes, I go.

I didn't say that.

No no no.

I'm lucky. I know it I do know it. I will never say it again think it again. I won't. Though it is so I don't know snake-like the way it gets in through the back of my head. But. Look at that man look at that woman all those people on TV in shops on the road look at everyone… It is okay. She is here she is with me. We are mother and daughter whether she remembers it or not whether I remember it or not.

And the good news—yesterday I know she knew me. For a second there she looked *at* me as if about to…then she forgot and my heart broke for me but more for her.

I imagine you among the falling leaves and the dry books in the library and the long walk back to your hostel room and the strange food you are forced to eat and the people you do not know—their accent and the lack of anything to laugh about—and I want to be there with you or you here with me or us somewhere altogether else.

I type 'Deb' on the screen and then sit there staring at letters three. I say it aloud. Deb. Look around. Deb, I say louder each time.

When are you coming? When? You say soon later this summer next year etc. and I go eat up my breakfast of… 'What did I eat in the morning?' I ask myself during lunch.

I live for this to be out in my little balcony barefoot in no shape to water plants or scrape bird poo off the railing. This is my moment my world my magic carpet mid-air. When I actually feel my soul somewhere in my body. I can't imagine not being here at this time of night when the moon is all mine mine mine. I imagine many people in many balconies stare at the sky right now this minute like me and the sky with every eye on it and how we are all in the end just each on his or her balcony small so small staring at the huge sky and the sky growing huger and us growing smaller.

An hour of this and my eyes give up. One morning when the doorbell rang I was sleeping here right here in this balcony without a sheet or pillow or anything and the sky gone all lights switched on and unrecognizable. I couldn't even look at it when I woke up it hurt my eye. But in the night it apologizes. Sorry it says with every star. Sorry.

I lose all control and write a long mail about how much how much I miss you how I cried because you forgot my birthday. You don't reply so I write again saying sorry in a tiny voice that I had no right to lose my temper that I know you are busy with your books and your term papers. And you reply saying hey missed your mail was caught up in semester end. A lot of parties. Sloshed. And happy birthday belatedly.

I took a printout of your reply memorized every word. Composed long and then short replies to it now droll now sober. I made this of it that of it. I want to demand you drop everything and come hold me once. Just once. And all would be sorted within my head and I would not have to think of this anymore. But you are not free and you are too far. You are there, I am here. Just because I have nothing to do I can't blame you for the slowness of time in the watch on my wrist.

I look different in the mirror a native of another land. Less me not-me me a me from the balcony made of night and nothing. My lips touch the glass just once I want it to kiss me back.

When I called out to you that first time a breeze had come and knocked the kite out of your hands. How do you know my name you asked still holding the string. Your mother told me. Downstairs when I asked her if she had a daughter my age as she stood amidst wooden boxes just out of a truck. You had just moved in.

Arms on hips you almost hit me for what I had done to your kite. My voice saying your name had released it like a soul.

I see the kite you know in the mirror each time I say your name. Tail up in the sky going down somewhere I can't see.

I used to leave the keys with your mother so I could see her every day. We'd talk about you what you must be doing feeling thinking eating. She is terrified you will eat meat and like it.

The day she locked up and left for your hometown she looked at me long shook her head and sighed as if to say 'if only'. I should have said then and there how much my mother had looked after me in her own time or that it was my duty to be there for her but I didn't.

I felt like I did once in a small-town carousel when the backward blowing wind had me gasp terrified because I couldn't scream or even breathe as I was choking right then on my own hair and had to pause the blind panic long enough to remember that it was only my hair to spit out one by one the strands stuck to the back of my throat. Only then could I scream.

Remember when we met just before you left for the US? Right in the middle of the road in that busy intersection next to the drugged baby in a beggar-woman's sling I wanted to bear hug the day. Just take in my arms and squeeze the life out of that one Sunday.

As we prepared to cross the road you took my hand grabbingly in yours against the blind batty buses and the zigzag people. Even before we reached the other side you removed your hand from mine.

THE FROCK

It was an evil little frock, by all means. Even at conception, even before its birth, this frilly fuss of multi-tiered flounces in scarlet satin and ruffled silk was a self-confessed monstrosity. The designer had wanted to impress. She'd had enough of her mousiness, her standard budget collection with discreet appliqué and embroidered hems, bought by women who aimed for quiet little daughters with impeccable manners.

The frock was an outburst, a riot of colours, a cessation of thought, a taking of the eye by storm. It began its existence on the pages of the designer's secret diary in self-important rustles and stage whispers, 100 per cent non compos mentis. As it took shape, the designer—whose mother nagged her on the telephone about her married lover and maimed savings—went ballistic in an attempt to shock even herself. No more sobbing on the kitchen floor drunk. Scissors high, it was her against tons of taffeta.

At the stitching stage the hired seamstress praised in sycophantic loudness. Oooh, she said. And aaah. But privately she gaped at the clash of fabric and hue, the vacuous flora and fauna of it, and worried about the soundness of her employer's mind. One night, blinded by the sameness of the infinite sequins in the frock's beehive bodice, she cursed its explicit unnaturalness. *Who* will wear this, she thought in defiance, all the while sewing furiously. *Who?*

Billowing high and low in the sanctum sanctorum of a state-of-the-art mall, the frock seemed to pucker up at passers-by. A child who tried it on sniffed the bejewelled collar, sprayed daily with cologne, and asked if flowers fart. A dress, the designer knew, was mostly about the settings: in the right place, under artful lamps, worn consensually, the frock would be all come hither.

Within months the frock had acquired an opaqueness she could not ignore. Instead of lifting the studio interiors with murmurs of imploding gaiety it began to cast a gloom, elongated shadows, brought roof closer to floor and rubbed the walls together. So when a corporate start-up came asking for possible prize donations the designer just unhooked it from the wall and handed it over.

The frock travelled in the back of an elderly Maruti van lolling against other trophies: eardrops in enamelled jade, coupons from a khadi boutique and three non-stick pressure cookers, large, medium, small. Wrapped in festive cellophane the frock was handed ceremoniously to the contestant voted runner-up at a beauty pageant. If she failed to return the cinemascope smiles of the tiara-topped winner during the long, mumbling speeches by the city's elite it was an ambivalence overlooked in the ululating nature of the day.

The frock demurred in the backseat tangling its tassels during the short drive home while the girl sat with her mother quietly, too quietly. The mother swept into their duplex, dragging her daughter by the sash. 'Try it on,' she said, coming to an abrupt stop at the dressing table mirror. 'Your *consolation* prize.'

When the daughter finished obeying, they turned to the reflection. The dress had inhaled the girl in the glass. Walking around her the mother fingered the fabric curiously, her heart set on the gratis nature of gifts rather than their utility. The organza sleeve rumbled audibly between thumb and index finger, crackling at such overfamiliarity. Her laugh a row of incisors, the mother said, 'Clearly for a fairer girl.'

Cast off, the frock slumped to its knees on the floor in classic slow motion. Through the night its fluted lapel swayed to and fro, humming menacingly, like the entrails of a half-eaten animal. In the early morning light, it gave the maid quite a fright before she composed herself with a squawk and folded it into a rambling heap on the dressing table. Later the mother gathered it up, cover and all, and threw it into the back of the cupboard much like she did all the other prizes her only daughter won.

Two years on, the family decided to move, two years that the frock spent nodding idly in the dust and darkness of the cupboard, mildew creeping up its hem. The woman had booked a bungalow in a gated community to live in relative isolation following her daughter's slit wrist. The frock sat on top of a box, half in, half out, wrestling out of its bubble wrap with single-minded rebellion, on its way someplace, one foot out.

'Madam?' the packers and movers enquired politely, pointing at it.

'*Throw it,*' shrieked she, also pointing at it. *Throw it. Throw it. Throw it.*

The men shook open the packet fully during tea break and the frock blew up like a homemade bomb in a marketplace. They fought it back kicking and screaming into the packet. According it the status of an invalid, their supervisor allowed the frock to recuperate at the warehouse on a bench of stone and lichen till such day a poor relative came asking earnestly for a loan and got stuck with it instead.

The frock boarded an express train headed south, only to be deliberately left behind in the second-class compartment, with spiced buttermilk soaking into its side and a 'fuck off' muttered in a rarely spoken dialect. Whereupon it launched itself at the train ticket examiner as if a toddler off a merry-go-round.

The TTE was habituated to picking up all sorts of left-behind souvenirs on the job. His wife though was equally adept at ducking these misbegotten mementos so that the frock cooled its heels on a shelf in the storeroom along with a jar of salted mangoes, torn out gift wrappings, plastic packets and a large bucket containing in it smaller buckets like paper cups for a giant's party. In the morning, sunlight made it through a wizened window near the ceiling. Sometimes a pigeon came looking for crumbs, its beak loud as gunshots against the rusted grill till it fell stupefied into a siesta on the ledge. Now and then someone came in and shook out a plastic packet or spooned pickle into a bowl. Once the daughter of the house came in, lit a cigarette, coughed and, looking around, stubbed it in a spangled detail of the frock. It burnt with a *sssss*.

The father brought a teddy bear next, man-sized and brown, from an AC chair-car. He laughed. 'I caught this fellow travelling ticketless!' The daughter stared blankly before throwing him and the teddy bear a practised smile of gush. Once a picture of her hugging the soft toy was taken he stretched on the sofa with a mini cushion at the nape of his neck and remembered the previous keepsake.

'By the by, where is that frock, the one I got last time?' he asked fondly.

'It is here somewhere,' said his wife, glancing at the clock; it was always too early or too late in the day for a squabble. Confectionary-coloured costumes, standing as they did for lisped good nights and climbing on to paternal laps, were the last thing the family needed at this point. There were short skirts and push-up bras and late-night concerts and a tattoo at the small of the back that he did not know about his only daughter, not yet.

Next day after her husband left for work she darted into the storeroom and balked at what she first took to be multiple rips before she saw that the frock was merely sun-dappled, thank God. Picked up, shook out, brought out–she tapped a foot, waiting for the maid to show up. To whom she extolled its virtues and emphasized her own generosity in parting with such an extravaganza. The maid barely glanced at the frock, keeping it near the backdoor alongside her umbrella and footwear, where she usually placed any freebies allotted to her.

'Sevi, take a good look! Very, very costly,' she said from time to time to ensure gratitude, to incite the maid into working harder. Extra dusting was thrown her way, all windows and shoes and commodes had to shine like the sun. By the time Sevi frothed her coffee up and down in two steel tumblers the frock was fluttering its impatience in a pre-monsoon draft. Ribbons broke free and began to flap, pointing long non-knuckled crystal-encrusted fingers in every direction; there, here, there.

Sevi walked home dragging her feet with her chin angled low, the frock growing heavy in the bag like a grizzly bear waking up from a nap. The sole of a chappal came off, slap-slapping her ankle. She reached the shanty she lived in and plopped the frock on top of the black-and-white TV. Where it sat for a couple of months, ticking and tocking– its lace sash dangling much like a beloved pet's tail–on Tamil newsreaders and a Rajnikanth who punched villains and sang tenderly to women.

'Akka.'

Sevi sat where she was, a tight-fitting tear in each eye. Sight is such a prison; when open, eyes are always settling on bars and flat surfaces, seeing only what is, unable to reach beyond. To dream–to see into the future, into what could be, to what she wished there to be, and most of all, what she couldn't even begin to want–first and foremost eyes must close.

'Akka.'

Four years ago when a local NGO had taken over the matter of her daughter's education, Sevi had been bewildered. She hadn't been convinced of anyone's goodwill back then. Her child should grow with strong limbs and a strong back, she had prayed when pregnancy made her an outcast. Her mother took the opportunity to disown her and her father feigned ignorance. Nothing left for her mother but to disbelieve one of them, Sevi knew as she stole away one morning.

The bare land she squatted on gradually grew into a tin shed around her whilst, pregnant and retching, she managed to find work as a domestic help in an arterial area of the city. From six in the morning to six in the evening she cooked, scrubbed pots, starched saris, arranged the morning tiffin into miniature murals on a plate, brought back chamathu kuzhandai (the sticky-sweet kids) from school for their mothers, swept room after room after room, bathrooms extra.

The baby had arrived more or less on time and Sevi's days grew messier, more fibrous. She couldn't refuse the NGO offer just like that. Not when they arrived bang on her doorstep saying they would educate her baby and take care of its every need. During the school holidays the baby would come back to her, it had been explained: two whole months out of twelve.

'Akka.'

Those people had kept their promise and her baby came back to her every year with textbooks in gunny bags and a mouth full of English. How the neighbours' jaws dropped when they heard her talk! Of course they needled Sevi later: 'One has a child so it is there for you. Who will fetch water for you, look after you when you have a fever and obey your every word? Why have a child if you cannot make use of the child?' They smacked their temples and shook their heads.

But Sevi knew a girl's lot. Swollen hands from constantly washing dishes at posh homes and hotels. Varicose veins from all that standing around (since sitting was a form of disrespect wherever they went). Public lavatories built in a line closer to the tarred road where she'd need a torch at night. Bare-chested boys lounging around the municipality taps chewing blades of grass, whistling. No schooling beyond the third standard, if at all. And babies, lots of them, some dead.

On clear nights Sevi dreamt she and her daughter had bicycle tyres for feet. They pedalled everywhere, taking completely for granted how super-light they were. On waking up she spent a lot of time trying to weigh the lightness. Light as this, light as that, she thought all day. Light as the strands of hair that came away in her hand after a head wash...

'Akka.'

...Light as the earth spinning under her toe at the sound of that voice right this minute. Here she was at last, at Sevi's door, for sixty days straight, starting today.

'This is for you,' Sevi said in a rush, handing out the frock first thing. The initial moments of meeting after such a long time were always awkward, they both knew this equally.

Her daughter-sister hesitated against the tarpaulin. 'For me,' she said finally, not looking at the frock. Sevi started at once to serve all the savouries she had made through the week—rice flour murukku, chilli fries, banana fritters—and spoke non-stop about nothing at all while the frock sat by shooting sparks like a private sun.

MORNINGS

'Check out cloud number nine,' solicits an angel at the zebra crossing, her gossamer gown askew.

I am hopeless with directions, not airborne either. Finding cloud nine will take me forever, won't it? Spent two whole minutes locating the airy-fairy pssst in the first place since angels don't clap owing to silly mix-up with eunuchs and the scarcity of aerial shelves to lay down harps.

'Can the cloud be home-delivered?' I tuck in the grey running out behind my ears, pout a couple of cracked lips and face squarely the acidic moonlight.

But a rustle of wings indicates the celestial commercial is over and I am currently addressing thin air. What a nuisance these creatures are, all said and done, posting their 'Paradise' placards bang in the middle of nowhere. Holding high their banners and no deo—angels have armpits too.

Don't get me wrong, angels are alright in their place, but oh so useless when it comes to hard-core discussions. Because you can look right through them and their translucent souls when they offer takeaway heaven in a box. A slice of morality that gives you nothing but gas.

First the facts: you have a son and so have I. Your son. Juxtaposed against my son. And I remember that summer again. When the eardrop danced on your cheek. Some man placed it there, I remember thinking. Some man.

All I focused on then was your hands that wiped the morning sickness off my chin and chest, the tea that kept the nausea at bay and perhaps your feet as you scurried all over my home and hearth, straightening, fussing, cleaning, replacing. I watched you from my bed, bloated belly blocking view. After all, you were hired to serve.

Any eloquence now is belated, of course. At that time I was the incriminating mute prey you wanted me to be. Or else why did you move on and take those burnt-out eyes with you?

My whole world was crumbling, obsessing me with its cracks and strains; a second pregnancy, you see, and I sought you once again, someone to tide me over these unending months, to clean up after me. And this evidence, for it was that as you and your son trundle up the long winding path out of the darkness, of further sabotage, is unwelcome.

My husband's spitting image is my first thought.

'Is he yours?' I ask hesitantly, for I am fully prepared to kick-start my belief in coincidences. Anything can be explained away if one obtains the right words or talks long enough or loud enough or believes in God, any God from the many out there.

Your glance is steady, almost as if the wait has been on your part and is now officially over. I hungrily gaze at the boy despite some faint warning bell inside my head bidding me to avert eye. He stares back. This boy of...

'Four,' you supply, robbing intensely.

The Orphanage for Words 81

Ah yes, I remember how many years it is since I returned home with the detestable bundle of joy, my firstborn, and you vamoosed.

My feet shuffle backward to the crudely concocted door. You follow me out, scratching your face, a matter of dragging broken fingernail down eggshell skin, and all of a sudden the scraping surface of your skin is hypnotizing. Still I make my escape, for clarity needs six by six vision and there is too much light around here.

'Kindly adjust,' I am told everywhere, in planes, in buses, on streets, in families, even here in these private places deep in my heart where you've come calling in debts too close to the bone.

The night is long and cloaking, but it has claws, I can tell. Who knows what nook of the night will unsheathe them? Who are you to cross the night? I mean, who are you? Angels are asses, disappearing before you ask for aspirin.

Your stricken face splinters and swims around me like photocopies of different sizes, as if that was all you awaited, my knowing, but all I knew at that moment was that this was a knowledge I could have done forever without, it so dovetailed with other not-knowings.

My head tilts up, sizing up the stars strung out like washing in the sky when a stampede from the opposite direction meets me formally. I wonder at the sudden influx of people streaming against me, at me, through me, dancing violently, followed by a horse carrying a flowered man. Ah, a bridegroom.

'Keep walking, you bitch, keep walking, or prepare to break out into blasphemous feathers,' the anti-angel brigade bids me and I hurry along the thorny brambles. It is a con-job, this paradise these prudes go on about. If my aches make them angels, let the parasites out of my heart. I shall ache no more.

'What use has goodness been to me?' I ask him from a roadside booth, clutching the phone tight, reading graffiti.

'Where are you?' he wants to know while the pane tells me: 'fukking u now'.

I nervously toss the receiver at the booth guy and collapse on a rickety stool. It comes upon me that I am no individual. Nothing so lofty as bone, brain, breath and blood. I am composed instead of extreme virtues, dripping with them.

He appears in a flash.

'My husband,' I greet without recognition.

He grabs my elbow, guides me back home, tucks me into bed, head aloft on a doubled-up pillow, and fluffs out the cotton under me until they are wings of white. I blink, but no, nothing so topical as a tear is under manufacture.

'Drink up,' he says, flashing his eyes at me. 'You are fine now.'

I try to swallow but the throat fights back. Sleep, however, has other plans; shoots morphine up my veins and hums a childhood tune, scattering me in the air.

Even if I shake off this insidious monstrous drowsiness, my body chooses not to obey commands.

It is the doing of those winged women, peeking and giggling at me from behind the curtain. Injecting soapy liquid to claw out mortal muck. I am so soiled and I can't fight anymore. With a flap of wings they have gagged and bound me in somebody else's body. The trick is to keep breathing.

But there is no marriage where they come from. They won't stay listening to wretched decisions that turn out all wrong in the end. After all, straying husbands bring on all kinds of debate. For. Against.

I know he is watching me. Behind these walls his heart beats, affecting endless patience. Crave quiet and it is granted with a vengeance. I haven't passed out in a drunken stupor; this is no happy hangover, because alcohol only makes me silly. I sense a light overhead, dizzyingly darkening the rest of the room. I want to crawl into the brightness and curl up within, so I can look down.

Bodies are known to go mute on you. Like now, when all feels see-through. I can hear no heartbeat, no scream in my throat.

'Nothing will matter anymore,' he vows as the milk dribbles down my chin and cramps unfold deep in my belly.

What doesn't? And when did they matter?

I think these words and I say them aloud but they turn against me even as I say them. Try to shift eyelids, stir tongue when he plucks the pillow from right under my head, the suddenness of his move giddying me.

I love you, he whispers.

It has the pallor of an open mouth, the pillow, like the sky come swallowing. Night has fallen, night has fallen, but mornings are overrated, aren't they?

BREASTS

I

It is late at night, almost morning. All lights on from electric to the moon. Everyone a little high. You just have to say something, anything, and everyone breaks into laughs. The two girls with us have to be dropped back to their hostel, their college hostel. They are first-year PU, wearing little skirts that they obviously bunched up at the waist—hanging uneven on their thighs—and smoking one cigarette between them.

'I hate that song,' said Leena in her little-girl way.

'I hate hates,' declared Ali grandly.

Leena looked at him uncertainly. Ali had just broken up with the love of his life and tended to be a little obscure. She had met him every day till her father came to take her back to Muscat. There she seemed to get along very well without Ali. Ali made it a point to flirt with every girl who came by.

Everyone predictably laughed. Leena laughed too, to show she was a sport. But he turned to her in an abrupt, angry movement. 'Come on, you don't really hate, do you? You can't love or hate a bit of music.'

'What do you mean?' She looked at her watch. 'It is late.'

'Late for what?' John asked. And this time Ali's laugh was loud and insulting.

The other girl, the one with a light moustache and sideburns, adjusted her glasses. 'Leena means...'

Ha ha ha, laughed John. 'Now you will tell us what Leena means? You are what, her secretary?'

'I am Koyal,' she said, hands on hips and very stern.

'Pleased to meet you, Koyal. Myself Ali.' The two boys laughed again. This time the girls did not join in. They looked at each other.

John said, 'If you ladies don't mind, I have little fairies dancing in my fly...' And casually scratched himself. 'Tell me,' he said conversationally, 'I have heard the girls in your college do it for money. Half touching five hundred bucks. Full touching thousand.'

'Don't be cheap!' burst out Leena, looking at the road back and forth, maybe to sight a cab or auto. But this part of town is deserted until you walk up to the choked marketplace and burst out into the open. Garbage spills over on both sides. We convinced the girls to come here as this pub is homey. Beer is priced way less compared to the ones on MG Road.

'They are not cheap, da,' John told Ali in a mock-serious way. 'How much do you have?'

'That is enough!' said Leena. 'Stop this shit, okay?'

John pounced on her, held her elbow and pulled her towards him. 'I am talking business. You said you don't like that song. I hereby promise not to play it ever, darling, if you can, you know, tell us your rates.'

I coughed. 'Leave it...'

'*Non mi rompere le palle*,' John snarled at me, adding obscurely, 'that's kind of Italian for fuck off.'

I tugged at Leena's other elbow, the one not in John's grip. 'Let's put them in a cab and that's it.' I panted in my effort to keep cool.

'We can't do a thing in a cab,' protested Ali.

'See, we are nice girls,' started Leena.

'We can't see if you don't show,' muttered John, and Ali asked, 'Nice girls means? You don't hang out with boys like us?'

'I mean...' she hesitated. 'I mean...'

'Oh, I got it!' exclaimed John and both girls turned to him eagerly. 'You don't fuck.'

They nodded slowly, not sure he meant it in a conciliatory way. I kept smiling at the girls, to show there was nothing to be scared of. I know Ali and I know John—they are decent people from decent families. Ali has almost completed his degree and John's uncle is a doctor in Manipal.

'Is that what you meant?' asked Ali.

The girls nodded.

'Say it,' ordered Ali.

'That is what we meant,' said Koyal in a bold voice.

'No, no,' laughed John. 'You have to say—we who never fuck.'

After a pause, during which I made a jerky movement but was quelled by a look from Ali, Koyal said in a dull voice, 'We never fuck.'

'So what do you do then?' John leaned forward, grabbed Koyal's elbow and repeated slowly, 'What? Do? You? Do?'

'N-nothing. Look, we need to reach back. The warden will notice us missing.'

'Of course you can go. In a bit. First tell us what *have* you done?'

'I have kissed,' said Leena quickly in a gasp.

'He kissed you or you kissed him?'

'He.'

'Tongue?'

She nodded, again quickly, as if to get it over with. But John let go of Koyal's elbow and crowded Leena against the wall. 'He did not touch you anywhere else? Really? You expect us to believe that, you slut?'

She flinched. His face was so close to hers, spit fell on her cheek. 'He wanted to... I didn't allow.'

Ali guffawed. 'She didn't allow. Did you hear that? *Allow!* How do you think the planet got filled if women did not allow?'

John held up an arm imperiously even as Leena whimpered. 'And you did not allow because?'

'He is not my husband.'

At this even I laughed. The girls looked at me accusingly. 'So you are the good girl who will do it only with her husband?' I asked. I think I had some vague idea that joining in will give me an edge and make it easier for me to put the girls into a cab and escort them back. I hoped to laugh at all this in say two minutes from now.

'I have to be in love,' asserted Koyal.

'Interesting that you say *you*. Because the man doesn't have to be, you know that. I mean he could be in love with you and not get it up just because he can't.' Ali puffed his cheeks. 'So then you would have to dump this man you love for a while and find another to make you happy.' He high-fived John.

'We are just a call away,' said John as if helpfully. 'But we have gone away from the topic.'

'Topic?' said Koyal.

'Of how far you have gone. What all have you done...'

'Oh God, will you stop this? You are freaking us!'

'Boobs?' asked John conversationally. 'Down there?'

Koyal nodded reluctantly. 'Which one?' he thundered.

She crossed her hands on her chest in answer.

'Okay,' said John, as if relenting. 'Show us some boob and we put you in a cab. Fair's fair.'

'Dream on!' said Koyal. But Leena stayed silent, a little glad that her breasts were not asked for.

'Quick!' said Ali. 'Don't make us mad.'

There was an angry hum in the air. The moon had stopped touring the sky and the lamp post seemed drunk.

'I won't!' said Koyal.

'Come on, a little boob won't hurt.'

'I won't!' She started to cry.

'You are wasting time, you know. You can keep on crying, but if you lift your T-shirt we can all go home,' John advised.

'I have only...' she hiccupped.

'Only two. We know that,' said Ali to John. 'God, I'd piss my pants if they had three. Or just one in the centre.' But she ignored him and continued to cry in earnest. Leena stood stiffly, as if she could cry too anytime if called upon to do so.

'We won't touch you,' said Ali in a fake tender voice. 'I swear on my...say, have you girls seen a dick?' This set John off on another round of laughter.

'Please don't rape me,' Koyal pleaded.
'Sister, I won't.'
'I am not your sister!'
'Then I might,' said John.
'Okay,' said Leena from her corner. 'Will mine do?'
'Both,' said Ali quickly. 'We meant to ask you both.'
'Can you leave her alone?' asked Leena.
'Why?'
'Because...one pair is like another. Won't mine be enough?'
'Okay,' said Ali after a pause of consideration. 'Show then.'

Quickly, in a trice, very matter-of-factly, Leena pulled up her top and along with it her bra by its bottom elastic. And suddenly there they were, the breasts; one, then the other, side by side.

It sobered everyone quick, I can tell you that. I wanted to blindfold Ali and John and I daresay they felt the same about me. Thing is the boobs we saw were not like the boobs in our heads when we were alone. These felt wrong to look at. Like small trusting things not made for this world. Like secrets told before their time. With veins like baby skies under the skin... They fuck you up, man, they do. Poems were coming up my throat like puke.

I think Ali sobbed one time, at least he made some noise like that, but when I looked he seemed okay. John said to me in a shaken voice, 'Drop them back, da.'

∽

II

No longer her warm old buddies, accepting a stray uplifting sock with rare grace. Just breasts. Pendulous. Luminous. Damaged. Soon to be a bosom more embedded than embossed. Who would want to be in her shoes? In her bra?

She stood at a magazine rack, staring blindly at the fare, when the prominent mammary on a glossy cover caught her eye. Inside she was sure there would be no picture of a one-breasted woman, like a pirate with a slipped eye patch.

She checked into the hospital on the coldest day in Delhi that winter.

'Nirvana Shah,' sentenced the receptionist. 'Room number twelve.'

'Like a sleeping pill?' asked a nurse the night before the mastectomy. The doctor had chosen the first day of the new year to greet her tumour in person.

'No,' she said.

Vana was in a mood to encapsulate. Her husband had all but moved out, with a tight-lipped explanation about some colleague who was abroad and needed his house watched. When she had seen him packing his stuff, for one crazy instant she had wanted to beg him to hug her. That was the day her tumour's true nature had been revealed to her. She had wanted to rip the rotting breast off, all 32 D of it. She had wanted to howl her heart out. She had wanted company.

By habit Vana fingered the lump. How would she sleep? She was going to be that princess who couldn't sleep because of a pea.

The Orphanage for Words 91

A nurse served pulao-raita. Setting the tray aside without tasting, she walked across to the room from where the TV could be heard. Watching the news all alone was a young man with his hand in a cast. With his other hand he manipulated the remote control. He looked at her. 'Is there anything else you want to watch? Except the new year shit?'

She shook her head.

They sat in silence and watched the havoc wreaked by war far away, heard depressing stats reeled out by cheery women in party clothes. The man in the cast was looking at her, she was sure. Out of the corner of her eye she confirmed that yes he was. Oh God! It was her chest he was staring at. She had not worn a bra and the night air had whipped out her nipples into two bullets under the flannel gown. Vana bent forward ever so slightly to slacken the fabric, her eye unblinking on the TV.

The man said, 'I am a photographer. Weddings, birthdays, funerals, indoors, outdoors…'

She nodded politely.

Faraway she heard the fireworks go. She glanced at the clock: twelve. Happy New Year. With one breast less.

And what if she forgot she ever had it, her second breast? Would she remember two, twelve or twenty years from now what it looked like, felt like, this breast with one foot out the door?

She began to unbutton the gown and asked the man, 'Can you click pictures with one hand?'

It was his turn to nod politely.

∽

III

Once upon a time long, long ago, L could not say breast and cancer together, not before the two settled down in her bra anyway. Today she is between breasts—one in exile, one under state surveillance. Between have and have-not. If you look closely it is like her chest is winking at you.

The disease was eating into her lymph nodes and her outer chest wall, the naughty thing.

Thank God, it is still to enter your inner chest wall, the doctor said during her last chemo.

Thank God, she echoed faintly, trying to recall gratitude.

Within a month the disease drew pistols—and impatiently submitting to tests and prods—declared war. It had been just a small lump in the beginning, something to tease and tweak. For a year L watched it grow almost like a third breast, stunted and shy. And then one day it oozed a clear white liquid.

'My breasts are falling like rotten fruits off a tree,' she wrote dramatically in her diary after the first chemo when she had griped idiotically about feeling too normal, too normal. Wait and see, the intern had warned and she had waited and puked buckets. Smells set her off, the sight of blood made her head spin. Mid-March her body behaved itself and a breast was consigned unsung into a bin.

But the chemo continued. Sometimes it felt to her that it always would, that it would continue long after her. Finding her vein was taking longer and longer these days so that her skin was blue denim. Stretched out on the narrow hospital bed with the needle up her arm, staring at the slowest ceiling fan in the world, she spelt out *brave* and *strong*—people called her that these days—till the words turned into inane anagrams.

It is only for about an hour that L can get everything right. She smiles serenely, skips a meal, handles a crisis phone call and gently raises eyebrows at the right places in a conversation. And then it is back to real life where tummy bloats, the loo is locked and she says the wrong thing and will never be spoken to again.

Skin gods, be kind, that used to be her prayer for long—pimples sprang up on her lips, eyelids, tip of the nose all year through. Now prayers were addressed to breast gods of every caste and country. She imagined the main breast god to be really a goddess made of multiple disposable breasts. And when this god laughed, which was often because men were always walking up to her and telling her funny things, the breasts stayed perky.

Hearing the words 'third-stage carcinoma' can bring on regrets—after the fatal shock that is. L's never had a baby. And at her age it is advisable really to just grin and go on. Still, when the doctor said the words, she worried about her future babies sucking at thin air.

She had imagined herself growing old with her breasts. They grew out after she was fourteen, they were supposed to live longer than her. They should have sagged and stretch-marked and lumped together in the middle, one day, looking unanimous.

People didn't know what to say to her.

A remembering of pain, a fear, an ache, a twinge in their knee, chest or groin that they'd like to forget forever, but which she kept alive with her own manifestation of their worst fear, that a tumour can bloom and take over like this.

So their faces are averted; please, they seem to be saying, just keep it to a telegram, your disease, your dirty smells, your diaper-clad bottom, and doctor said this and doctor said that. They have done their bit by arriving at your deathbed, do not expect them to now sing you a lullaby.

That's what cancer did to other people's faces, take normal everyday expressions and twist them into nothing anyone's ever seen. The doc's—when he lapsed into textbook phrases and scientifically exact language—resembled any ordinary vegetable vendor in a street corner explaining why the spinach was no longer fresh.

Friends thought she was going to drop dead right before them; in fact, in their faces she saw imminent death, her own. Poor thing, their faces said, you poor, poor thing, even as they listened to her small talk on the subject. Don't die right now, they seemed to implore, wait till we leave.

Then there were the offended faces of uncles and aunts and cousins and parents. And more importantly...how they never asked for the details, how they lived their entire lives skirting around her cancer, their faces stiff with the effort of speaking about everything else.

Cancer left her with no time. She stopped texting, savouring coconut water and TV shows. The only thing she did well was staring into space, for some reason a little to the left. Yes, this was the one thing she had not known about the big C, that it was a full-time job.

So here she was, very much aware of the advancing carcinoma in her system and having to underplay it, downplay it, play it cool, pretend the cancer was a little indoor game she liked to play when it rained outside.

Baby, he used to say on good days, you are something to hold on to. My flesh-and-blood woman.

As opposed to the bone and lycra ones? Thanks a ton.

But the big C came up against his soft-ons and he became ex, though she still thought of him in the present tense. Especially when she reached out for the phone and realized it had never rung.

L spends her time these days reading all the recommended literature and making all the usual promises to love her body through breast and through breastlessness. At home, in public places, while shopping for veggies or chatting on the phone, she often looks down. She finds herself doing this constantly, obsessively. She wants to see them up close, she wants to see them from a distance. She wants to see them in the third person, like they belong to someone else. My poor little chest, she sobs into hankies, into the exaggerated concern expressed by others. Suddenly the click of a bra hook is music to her ears.

Though bras are nothing but accomplices. Padded, seamless, stick-on, strapless, underwired, gel-filled, minimizing, straightening, framing, lacing, belting, pointing, expanding, muffling lumpy nipples or launching them into space...L's love-hate relationship with her breasts had begun one rainy day when she was still waiting for her body to, well, grow. It was in a dark alley on her way home from school that this shapeless creature had advanced towards her padded chest. He tugged at one water-soaked sponge and when it came off twang into his hands he thought he had amputated her in his overenthusiasm. His expression had been more horrified than hers.

Of course bras could be real bastards and suddenly decide to put in papers. Many a time, L had exhaled hard only to feel the elastic bungee jump off her ribcage. Usually this happened while facing elderly and bespectacled members of the opposite sex in academic corridors. Then she had to find the nearest private place to put it back on.

Meanwhile bills were mounting. Every damn thing cost the earth. Even the cabbie who took her to and fro robbed her blind. The insurance people wanted minutiae that took her forever to transfer into forms.

She moved into a friend's farmhouse—the friend was abroad and asked her to live in, an offer she couldn't refuse. At first all that infinity had an alienating effect. She stood awkwardly with one toe digging into the imported carpet, longing for the cramped interiors from an earlier life. It was odd, the way roominess can renegotiate issues of occupation. She had to rise to the challenge of capaciousness, to conquer the profusion before her before she could enjoy such plentitude of...nothing, of spying no material object as far as the eye could see, of stumbling over space and more space.

While the garden in the front flaunted flowers she couldn't name in gay abandon, the backyard toiled in studious harvest. The daily yield of beetroots, pumpkins and other seasonal vegetables travelled tastily to the dining table courtesy an overpaid domestic staff. As L spooned in the fare, she could visualize the fresh-faced warmth of each vegetable inside her. When she stretched out on the swing on the back veranda and patted her stomach she could almost touch her sun-dappled intestines.

Skipping along Khan Market, L juggles the stole at her shoulder, playing unintentional hopscotch, as people blinded by sun or shopping aim to walk bang into her. She surveys not the sunglasses, sausages and saris on display, but her own silhouette from shop window to shop window. Here and there she stops to gaze into a display, pretending deep interest in a jazzed-up camera or a wee shirt for a beach-bound tot, but in reality eyeing her body's new profile. Even her shadow has had to adjust she notices.

She wishes some man would appear from nowhere, walk her down a café, seat her on a wooden bench and feed her cake. He must be entirely nonsensical, make no mention of politically grave matters or latest medical advances.

In the boutique's dressing room she takes on the mirror. And zooms in on the *enemies*. Ever since they grew out, she had been telling herself forget them, just forget them. But they had been right there, under her very nose, pouting, swelling, taking over with such sly arrogance that with every breath they made their move. The more panicky she got the harder she breathed and the more they inched into view to taunt, destroy.

Earlier she never looked if she could help it, opting for furtive darts, hoping against hope that this shirt or that with the huge pressed-down pockets in the front would manage to suppress the mutinous two. She used to invest in scarves and jackets, disbelieving of women who blew themselves up with silicone.

L whips off her shirt but hesitates to pick up the untried cherry-red top. She throws her hands up in the air as if at the approach of an old friend and watches the spot from where she has been scooped out. The hollow ebbs and flows with blood and broken blue veins, puckering inward like a pricked balloon. In sleep when she forgets and her hand falls to her chest it disconcerts her at first, that there's no party going on. Then she lets her hand lie flat on her heart. It reassures her, the sweet rustle of hush.

What to call them had always been a dilemma when she was growing up and these damn things took residence on her body, making it impossible to flash anyone. Breasts, tits, knockers, jugs, boobs...all seemed so demeaning or clinical. With one down and one more to go, she was still wondering what to call a breast gone solo.

She told a woman in the outpatient department that she'd name them Amitabh and Jaya. But soon Amitabh would step down and Jaya will bag a double role, the woman said. Besides that's such a *planned* name, like trying to play down or up or something. But how can you name someone you can't see anymore? Or rather someone no one else can see, only you can.

L throws back her shoulders. Out comes the phantom breast to play. The one that doesn't rhyme with anything, can't be heard or seen, doesn't pat her heartbeat like it used to. She ducks the blonde woman's elbow aimed at her... what? Damn, she must name it.

Monkey darling. It comes to her late at night, between a toss and a turn, when one side of her body heavy with flesh rolls down the empty other side. What she had loved and hated and bathed and bad-mouthed for so long.

L sits up slowly in the bed and touches her chest tenderly. What can you say about mammary made up of moonlight and mist and memory and mangled skin? Monkey darling, she sings. My own monkey darling.

DOG

We had barely sat down for breakfast that day when a strange whistling sound sailed down our fifth-floor window.

'What was that?' we asked simultaneously, staring at each other before rushing to the wide window. Heads from other windows were peeping down anxiously too.

'Oh, it is that dog,' said the domestic help in a disappointed voice.

A pavement splattered with a mongrel's mortal remains was a comedown for her. She would have preferred something gorier than a mere canine corpse. We returned to our breakfasts with diminished appetites. The omelette no longer felt fluffy and the tea turned metallic. Everything tasted…dog.

'Whatever possessed it to jump?' a next-door neighbour asked, walking in without greeting or apology. 'It was from the seventh floor. The whole night it yelped and yelped. Then at 9 a.m. sharp, it just jumped.' He shook his head. 'I have informed the building secretary. If not cleared up immediately the stink will be unbearable.'

'I am glad it is dead though. These municipality people do nothing about stray dogs in the first place,' my husband grumbled. 'This last week I counted at least five mutts here. And then of course the more common they are, the hastier they breed.'

In his bedroom my son tried to keep his eyes shut, but it was a futile exercise. On holidays he is allowed to sleep all he wants and get out of bed at his own whim, but the bright morning sunshine combined with the ominous thud downstairs made further sleep impossible. The maid went in. 'You will never believe what happened. A dog just committed suicide.'

In a trice he was up. 'I hope it wasn't Browny? Was it a brown doggie? Oh, please say it wasn't Browny.'

She led him ceremoniously to the window. 'Look,' she pointed down.

'It is Browny,' he wailed. 'Someone has pushed her down! Now whom will I play with?'

He ran to his father. 'Papa, why is my Browny still lying there? Why hasn't she been shifted to a hospital?'

'It is dead. And it is only a street dog,' he consoled.

'Have you cleaned your teeth?' I asked

'Mommy, do you think she is really dead?'

But I was in the next room by then and pretended not to hear. He rang up his friend whose parents were doctors. 'Could you come over, please? There is a very sick dog here.'

I ran out, snatched the phone from him and spoke apologetically into it. 'It is not ours... Dead... Yeah, I know... I am so sorry... You know how children are.'

Barely had I put the phone down when he made another call. This time to a friend who lived in the same building as ours. 'Browny is dead, aunty. Can I speak to Shweta?'

'She is sleeping.'

'Just tell her Browny…is no more.'

I was firm with him about having to go to the bathroom. Throughout the cleansing ritual he informed me about the late dog.

'She had eight pups, you know.'

I knew because he had pleaded to be allowed at least one as a pet.

'Of course, only two are left.' He spat some foam into the basin philosophically. 'Who will look after them now?'

'Breakfast…' I began but he had already started down the stairs to where the dog lay. I followed in a hurry, running all the way, close behind to prevent him from touching the carcass. It was a filthy dog, after all. Who knew where all it had been? Also, his pajamas were buttoned all wrong.

The dog lay sideways, pretty much the same way we had espied it from our flat above.

'Don't touch it,' I said urgently, but he had already bent down and scratched it gently behind an ear.

'Sleep all you want, Browny.'

HEARTS

Men. They were going to kneel around her in a circle so she'd wear a skirt entirely made of men one day.

Only to this end did M invoke the spirits of dead femme fatales. Who came haunting on high heels, these bad-girl ghosts, mostly as she had pictured them, with mussed hair and not a stitch on them. Pale wraiths with slit wrists, tarts and trollops with their panty lines showing, sultry sirens blowing smoke, mistresses and keeps with arch smiles, sex kittens, harlots and size-zero starlets, chasing up cads and cocktails, with come-hither eyes and lips in a moue.

'Make me,' she begged them, 'you.'

Strung along all her adult life with promises of muscle tone and a swan-like neck, she was applying for change, body and soul. She'd pray for world peace when she was beauty queen, but right now, God knew, she needed some oomph.

In a strange city M was initially sidetracked by job-related minutiae, a new breed of insolent button-bursting women at work, the pandemonium of peak-hour traffic, and the eerie turmeric-smeared face of her landlady popping up when least expected. On her birthday she bought a cake, cut it and ate it all by herself. No man to share it with. But sometimes one is happy not having to share. Especially cake.

So many yeses and so many nos in so many hearts, male and female, gooey and liqueur-filled. Her fingers itched to run through hair, and her hair itched for fingers to run through it. By her window, in a low chair at midnight, she practised sitting in a man's lap. She grew pale and uninteresting, ate poorly and ailed deep in her heart, her hymen alone healthy as a horse. She could kill herself or travel abroad but she was big-boned and the rupee too weak.

∽

'Can I help?' offered a new colleague the next day at work, with a grin so perfect he could only be a salesman of teeth.

As she surrendered her PC, she noticed a mass civil disobedience movement in her entire being. She watched each of his facial features separately and raptly as if at fireworks in the sky. Such merry eyes! She had visions of Santa lurching in the snow, eyes stolen. M went *nnnnng* like a bell in the head. Felt she could shop stark naked for hours. Or sit through ten root canals straight without anaesthetic.

In the office canteen, stale sandwiches felt like songs in the mouth. He who had come from another country and would return soon was deeply absorbed in all she spoke and stammered. When he tucked a runaway lock of her hair behind an ear, she felt the ear quietly explode. The proximity of his palm to hers on the tabletop made her eyes wide and wondrous like in a Manga strip. She must, she just must, steam him open!

He dropped her home that day and en route got her some roses. It rained a little; she wanted to fly to the sky and lick it dry. Inside her were water lilies and ducklings quacking sonatas.

The car reached her lane and they bid goodbye to each other like any other couple. She stood there smiling very, very slightly so her nose remained slender and any food stuck between her teeth didn't show. He stuck his forehead to the window as the car pulled out and it was very wistful, that face in the window.

That night in her dream when Gabbar Singh tied him to a pole she danced on broken glass to secure his release.

Next morning she gazed rapturously at her office building. Feeling small and vaporous enough to be bottled like a genie she lunged towards it with lunatic joy.

It was strange, M reflected, how three decades could be a blink when you met the right person. Quake-proof and suddenly, boom, 9.9 on the Richter scale.

Table for two. Angel hair pasta in a cheese corset. Wine that strummed the tongue. There was no denying it, she had a thing for forearms. She'd seen smiling wrists on men just like she'd seen cross ones. Sometimes their elbows went straight to her knees.

He laced his fingers with hers and she felt for the first time the deliciousness of a hand in hers. From shoulder to fingers five, a hand all hers to hold.

He raised their clasped hands to his mouth. 'I feel urgent about you.'

'Urgent,' she echoed, 'what a beautiful, beautiful word,' and rubbed his cheek with a piss-drunk hand.

'I need a shave.'

She shook her head though she'd have liked to clarify it was not stubble per se she liked but *his* stubble. Stubble without him under it would just be overgrown hair poking out of the skin of somebody's cheek.

She placed her mouth on his and almost jerked back. What an alien unaccustomed thing it was, another mouth. Could she convey her lust, her liking, her limitations in so mundane a manner, with a mere mouth? She would have stood still as a statue forever if his lips hadn't at that precise moment begun to stir.

Bluebirds flew out of her ears. Daffodils sprang under her nose and all was melodious fragrance. M, who had never been kissed, found that a little kissing was a dangerous thing. That until the earth split open or the sky fell out, two mouths could ask for nothing more than to mash each other up.

'Come,' he said.

'Follow that man,' she told her feet.

She hugged him and in that hug, she held her heart. Stomach to stomach they stood, very cream biscuit. Her nipples, he said, were tall, dark and handsome. This was what it boiled down to between men and women. Pure want. The thick unassailable insoluble centre of all heterosexual urges; everything around it, the soft taffy and the caramelized candy, sucked to sweet spit. Inter-heart, all languages left behind. And a secret was born between him and her, a secret roughly their combined size.

In the morning, he ran a finger down her nose. 'Go straight down and turn left,' she guided him to her heart. The world had calmly destroyed itself around them while they slept and he had inherited her.

'It is 5.30,' he said.

She nodded, unwilling to crawl out of the red juicy plum she had been sleeping in and supping on like a snug-smug worm. He said he'd call her and she wanted to clap her hands, to applaud the way their eyes met. The way only their eyes could meet surely.

∽

First month she tried, she really tried, to be busy, to distract herself, to not stare at cellphone, clock, calendar. He is taking it slow, that's all. But even after she had tended to work and fingernails, answered mail and doorbell, boiled milk and eggs, oiled hair and scootie, flipped pages and channels, there was this surplus of her, one foot tapping, waiting. Shakuntala live. She was her own mythology.

Second month she remembered details. The kisses, the touches, the giggles, the sweet and sour of him. All the while his roses drooped and shed black petals… Monologuing passionately into her pillow, asking only for this terrible silence to be broken, she grew desperate for an antidote to him.

Third month she felt raw and exposed, nowhere to hide. You were too easy, said the voices, you gave it away for free. Why will he come back, for what? For me, she whispered, but it was a tinny whisper.

Fourth month she feared he had died, that his corpse was lying unidentified in some government morgue with his mobile ringing continuously under the regulation blanket. He was, in her mind, a mass of missed calls from her. Inside her head was him and her with fingers linked so long so strong they'd fossilize eventually for future archaeologists. Inside her head was total crap.

The Orphanage for Words 107

Heartbreak, she found, was on prepaid. Vampire bats dashed against her chin and chest, searching for her vein, her neck. Derailed, denuded, deluded, deserted, demolished, damsel in distress, and that was only D. Asphyxiated, bereft, contused, egg on face, forgotten, gutted, hyperventilating, ill, jagged, knuckle-rapped, let down, maimed, negated, over and done with, pulped, quieted, rotting, short-changed, tainted, unhappy, vandalised, witch-hunted, x'd, yellowing at the edges, zonked...her new A to Z.

Weekends were devoted to crying jags. The storm after the calm. Outbursts of anger and petulance against the world that pressed against her nose like a sheet of glass, outbursts to make the Mon-Sat sojourn bearable. Sundays were her day to frantically clean the toy-sized flat, but when a trick of lighting at sunset turned her walls to brocade she broke down all over again. Crying, she found, was when all the emotional turned irrevocably physical, each organ in a separate hell. How the heart held the body hostage!

If it had been cancer or a relative's death, she could mourn for all to see; she wouldn't have to be furtive, huddle in back alleys, wear gloves and go undercover. A fracture would mean sick leave and hospitals and visitors with baskets of fruit, but this hairline crack in her heart had to heal on its own.

And the relentless moving forward of life and living. Of putting the washing out to dry. Of retail therapy without lists, taking untold risks in shampoos, groceries and undergarments.

Though she seemed to loiter and linger and lurk, all the while she was frantically planning elaborate trysts in the bedroom of her mind. Detail was her joy—what he wore, what she wore, when they cast these off—though she was stymied now and then by the solidity of walls or people going the other way. Sorry, she'd say automatically, only to find her fantasy gone and her index finger hovering mid-air where previously his nose had been.

Her legs grew lax and, hurried on as if by effete horsemen, her feet fell behind. She began to walk with her knees slightly splayed, like she harboured gynaecological secrets. She had often heard people say FO but never studied how someone actually fucked off. So undocumented and little known, this act of fucking off. Now told to FO, she relied on blind instinct, on gut feeling, to go with the flow. Of FO.

She sought refuge in public toilets marked 'Lady', 'Woman', 'She' or 'Her'. I am going to Her, she'd announce to no one in particular and dart in to bawl.

She had to leave, he had already waved farewell. All that was left was to smile politely and say okay then, see you around, no, no, I have my own transport. Back to my own life.

∽

She had hard-core fantasies about his death. Something inexplicable and bulky coming down on him, like his roof. Face crushed but incandescent under the chandelier. Succumbing to venereal disease so new, so fatal, they'd name it after him. Fed so much poison, his pee is India's leading export in pesticides.

Falling in love had aged her. Rejection was why, M realized belatedly, some of her colleagues had that weather-beaten, hard-eyed, used look. That was how the rebuffed half coped, by closing down their face, those parts of it that gave away secrets. A woman with a past, she had become that.

'Yes,' she screamed down someone at work, 'I am a fool. I am your basic A-level fool. Stand next to me for instant upgrade. I make anyone look good!'

The other girl scurried away with her hands up in mock surrender, pretending to be a poor little thing.

Still, her outburst was the talk of the office, and for hours afterwards it elicited comment around the coffee machine. M was aware of the covert glances, the almost-awe she had inspired. A watermelon had once burst of ripeness in her house and its sweetness and seeds had scattered into a distance. There was the sound of a gunshot–bang!–and the most inaccessible of corners were sprayed with fruit. You can't be too full of anything, not even sweetness, it would seem.

M emptied bowls of candied cherries, bought a roadside book on combating depression, watched the butcher chop plump animal limbs into bite-size pieces, and gradually steadied her pulse rate. It was all right, she told herself. It was just a matter of...

Time vs right now

Head vs heart

Self-help books vs chick lit

Once she had grasped the truth–every dog may have its day but every day has its dog–there was no mistaking her determination to heal. With the gilt of chocolate wrappers crackling under her feet, she wallowed in home truths. She had to care for him two hoots:

1. Hoot.
2. Hoot.

Um, change the order please, 'table for two' to a 'coffin for one'. Pollyanna died. The police just called. Head-on collision. Didn't feel a thing.

Being fobbed off, by and large, was not what she objected to, it was not being consulted. By withdrawing wordlessly, he had sprung hierarchy upon them.

But where do you report the loss of an unsung hymen? A lifetime of innocence and trust and sweet hope in one size that fits all? He was supposed to return, to return to tell her he cannot return.

All the bad-girl ghosts began to jump up and down inside her, pouty and petulant, stamping their spiky stilettos, baying for blood. M addressed them first of all: 'Scram, girlie ghouls!'

Geishas froze, full of grace. Sirens got sore throats, averting shipwrecks, letting all the pretty sailor boys get away. Zombies plunged back into the warm wormy earth, lap dancers scrambled off male laps and yelped for mommy laps, yakshis could hold a tune no more. Only the banshees wailed.

Crumpets and strumpets, hussies and harpies, not bashful anymore but deeply diabolical monkeys full of mischief. Floozies and slags counting all their money; there was no pleasure in prostituting slammed against a grimy wall without this jingle and this jangle. Hookers, beware, hard cash instead of the stupid, stupid heart every time. Baring claw and maw, twitching a serpentine tongue, the bitch blew her nose.

It was on a full-moon night that every drop of M's blood turned werewolf. Hate, like love once had, arrived unconditional. Hate, love—no one slogged for these. It was just there, bam. Like calcium deficiency. Or a blood group.

In her first act of anarchy, her former beloved became 'Littleshit' on her phone. She practised witchcraft on cacti. *I wish you dead. I wish that six months from now someone will tell me you died on this day, this hour, this minute.* Women may have meant him harm before, but she had something they all lacked: a black tongue. She opened her mouth, stuck out her tongue—aaaaah. Nice and black. Okay, she amended. Let's begin small. She wished him itchy scalp, falling hair and lots and lots of dandruff. She smiled in her sleep, dreaming of black collars turning white every time he shook his head.

She had been the dunce of every man's dreams, fired after fellatio, curtains on opening night. Embarrassing herself with impromptu flashbacks was handy in keeping her on track. If she did not inject a little venom now and then into her veins, she might find herself ridiculous. And that ridicule may become an antonym to the hate, and she may reverse-pedal the vicious cycle and end up back at the aching and the hankering and the beauteous beginnings of them. Before tear no. 4,361—the very last tear—rolled down her cheek. Before the spreadeagled legs and the sweet nothings and that first primal scream of a stare.

To slay her dragon she invoked all her childhood heroes—Jhansi ki rani, Chacha Chaudhary, Mandrake, Phantom, Hanuman and gadadhari Bheem. She was all of them against a single solitary man. A clap of thunder made her start. 'Shake loose a shower just for me,' she coaxed the clouds. She must reoccupy herself. Even the roses were looking down on her! She put them into a plastic bag and threw them in the garbage chute and the room was haunted no more by a perfume past.

A murmur grew within her till she herself was a murmur. Murmurmurmurmurmur, she went, murmurmurmurmurmur. Running after the pigeons once with murder in her heart—the defecating-everywhere, egg-bombing pigeons—thinking, I'll cook you and feed you to the pigeons. A murmur the pigeons respected.

Revenge grew from a little daydream in the corner of her mind to the 3-D vehemence of cinematic vengeance, an OCD capable of afflicting up to ten scorned women at a time. She'd be his personal fishwife.

∽

But.

What if memories were inventions of a deserting mind? What if the things she thought he said and did were what *she* said and did? What if she willed him to say/do what he said/did? After all, it was only a word or two, a touch or two, and in a whole cosmos of words and touches spoken and touched and still being spoken and touched everywhere, what were a word or two, a touch or two?

Such opportunists they'd been, highlighting her 'goodness' against his 'badness'. If he had deceived, so had her ears. What business had skin retaining throbs well past the touch? When the rose-plucker's thumb was pricked the thorn's cry went unheard. Speech and touch were provocations of the moment, living in the moment for the moment. Tick-tock, gone. Skin, go back to peaches and cream.

She remembered too his abrupt silence, the lack of words that turned her homicidal. The hunger to have and to hold but no having, no holding. The no-rains, the no-calls, the can't-eats, the don't-dos, the no-nos, really, the nothings... Why *did* the mind fixate on nothings?

Served her right, for thinking his defection the end of the world. She was only thirty-something, for God's sake, there would be other cheats, other catastrophes. Staking her all on what? A tingle at the base of her spine? She conceded how her one moment of confidence in an entire lifetime of cowardice could be seen as bold.

And, well, morality. Could she really accuse him of turning her into one of those? A loose woman. A fallen woman. As if women were teeth, to loosen and fall. He had been a bad choice. But *choice*. And had delivered exactly what she demanded of her future back then. To be wanted.

She had longed for someone vaguely like him for so long, and she had longed for a speech chosen only for her with words so tender their backs broke as they surrendered their meaning. But then people ran into each other because they simply couldn't sit at home all day. They paid fake compliments, smoked and coughed, and laughed delightedly at bad jokes. Then, at some point, all of society needed to be pared down to one. Someone to take home and screw the hell out of.

One man coming up. Man gone, case closed. She honestly couldn't mentally replay what they had done together, she and he. Two soap bubbles bursting at first touch. '*There is no us, no etymology of us. We can't be coded, catalogued, compared or filed for future reference. We, except for that brief moment in my head, did not exist.*'

She concluded that the next time, if there was a next time, there would be a safety net—of a formal engagement and parental blessings—when it came to men. Perishables like love and lust are best refrigerated in marriages. She would play the game society's way. That way when he fled they'd chase after him and club him to death.

She'd party like her aunts and grandaunts. Who bumped their husbands off early with high-cholesterol diets of all kinds of meat from day one, and now lived alone in their huge rose-ringed bungalows and giggled through church-planned trips to the Holy Land every year with other widows.

For now, between the dizzying heights and the doldrums, a desired domicile called Survival. Men may come and men may go but most women had only one head. A brief stopover in la-la-land and now she must return. All rebels in No-Nonsense Land were granted amnesty, she'd heard it that morning on the radio.

Perhaps all practical women began as impractical little girls.

That night she slept deeply. Gabbar still tied men to a pole in her dreams but she refused to budge despite being a renowned dancer with two right feet.

DOLL

'Are they twins?' Mala asked. She was like that, easily excited. That, in fact, was the best thing about her. How her face had glowed when she first met me!

'Mommy, tell me, no. Are they twins?'

Mala's mother snorted. 'I don't know. Just behave yourself. They are, after all, the children of your father's boss.'

And off she went to organize the pastries and drinks. She hated it when someone ate at her place and did not ask, 'From where did you get *these*? They are heavenly/delicious/to die for.'

She wouldn't say anything at the time, just smile slightly. But later she may allow Mala to hug her, and not notice how dirty I am.

'Twins! Did you hear that, Dolly?' Mala jabbered to me. There was nothing she did not tell me.

I tried to smile back enthusiastically, but I was thinking how where I was born there had been hundreds like me, with the same red frocks and black button eyes. We had been hundreds of twins there. Of course, I was lucky to have met Mala almost immediately.

That evening the sisters came. They were twins, but sadly for Mala, not identical. Being a well-brought-up child she dealt bravely with her disappointment.

One of the girls pointed at me, hooting. 'You have a doll!'

Mala's mouth wobbled. 'No, no,' she said. 'This is an old one we have kept around just so some baby visitor can play with her.'

'Her? You call it a her?'

'See, I have a new computer game,' Mala distracted them and I heaved a sigh of relief. I hate to see her put in a spot like that. At nights when she hugs me, she always apologizes for such insensitivities on others' part. Even her mother hates to see her dress me up or sing to me. 'Go out and play,' she'd yell at Mala.

There was a woman employed just to play with Mala the whole day. Sometimes, when Mala's mother's friends came home, she'd say, 'Baby ko leke jao.' And we'd all troop out, me perched on Mala's hip. In the parking lot outside, the woman chatted with other maids while Mala chatted with me.

Once, just once, Mala's mother stopped her from taking me along. Mala missed me so much she cried all the time she was out and I missed her, too. Especially when immediately after Mala left, her mother burst into tears and told the guest how difficult everything was ever since she had a child. But wait until you hear what happened next. When Mala's mother went in to change, the man blew his nose with me. The indignity of it!

Next day, sure enough, Mala's mother yelled again how dirty I was. She is always dunking me in the washing machine. I don't mind the hygiene, but she could at least wait until Mala is in school. She cries each time I go into the machine. She presses her nose against the glass while I go round and round in the soapy water.

These washes keep me clean, and I am happy to be clean, but they also exhaust me. My hair and clothes get raggedy each time. Not that Mala minds and she is the only one I want to please. But in the last wash my mouth came off. My mouth! It was actually a red thread stitched above my chin in a broad 'U' to make it appear like I am always smiling, which is why I couldn't stop grinning even when that man blew his nose.

But whenever Mala came home from school, or her parents went out leaving her alone, she'd always look at me and smile. I was always smiling, you see. But with that red thread gone, I looked surly. Or sad.

Mala noticed it straightaway. 'Dolly's lost her lips!' she cried. The ayah started to laugh at that. What's so funny, I wondered. Would she laugh if it happened to her? Could she laugh at all without her lips?

Mala's parents had gone for a party. Mala's mother usually went to and came back from the parties happy. She always mentioned meeting at least three people who did not, would not, could not believe she had a child.

It was midnight when Mala's parents finally came home. She had waited up for them, just so she could tell them about my lost smile.

'Mommy, papa,' she called.

When they did not respond she went to their bedroom with me, saying, 'Look at Dolly's face.'

Mala's father glared at her. 'Why aren't you asleep?' Then he glared at his wife. 'She doesn't look like me at all. One of these days I'll get the truth out of you, if I have to kill you.'

'Go away,' Mala's mother told us. She did not look happy. I think someone finally believed she had a child.

Ayah has been asked to leave. She was caught stealing, Mala's mother said. But I heard the cook tell the press-wali that Mala's father had hugged Ayah, which is why Mala's mother told her to go.

Ayah packed her small bag and was about to leave. She had reached the front door when she noticed me in the foyer. Mala leaves me leaning there in the showcase, so that I am the first one she sees on opening the door when she comes back from school. From here she carries me to the dining room where I watch her eat. Then she puts me in a pram and wheels me about, telling me in detail every single thing she did since she left home. There is even a small cradle in which Mala rocks me to and fro. She always sings while doing this.

Ayah stood there looking at me for a long while and I wished I could smile goodbye. Then she walked toward me and very deliberately plucked out my eyes. Yes, my eyes! After that my world went black.

I am one of those dolls without nose or eyebrows to begin with, so lips and eyes were all I had and now they were gone. I sat there blindly waiting for Mala, waiting for light.

Ages later, I heard the door open. It was Mala's mother. She called out to the cook. 'Woh gayi?' She meant Ayah. The cook must have nodded, as I did not hear her speak.

Then Mala's mother muttered, 'This doll, I tell you, what a nuisance! Why can't Mala play with her expensive duty-paid foreign dolls? Why must she drag this ugly thing all over the place, making me a laughing stock?'

'Throw it before Mala comes,' she told the cook. 'Tell her, the maid stole it.'

I was put into a plastic bag. Damp tea leaves and muddy coriander stems clung to me everywhere. Then the plastic bag began to rock to and fro like the cradle Mala sometimes put me in.

Where was the cook taking me, I wondered. And then it struck me.

There have been dark whispers about such places in the toy factory. That this was how we dolls met our end. That we all ended up in the municipality garbage dump. I did not want to go there. I wanted to see Mala.

'How baby cried!' I heard the cook say to someone. 'But they have got her another doll from Singapore. Such blue-blue eyes and golden-golden hair.'

My last thought as I sailed into the black hole was that Mala would *never* forget me...

THE SOFA

Her shoulders are shaking. I know without looking that my daughter-in-law is amused. I was sitting on the sofa and peeling off my sock when the skin of my foot came off along with it. I said loudly, oh my God my foot has come off because that's what I thought had just happened. Later I saw it was only the skin.

This set her off. She is thinking, what a foolish old man. But when she turns around and sees my foot I know she will stare at it with delicate disgust, shudder and go to her room to recover.

After my evening walks I often soak my feet in hot water. The maid—employed by my son to look after me because, you see, I'm such a tough job really, and no one, especially my daughter-in-law, can be expected to do this—used to say the water is hot, it had just been boiled etc. But when I'd dip my feet I'd find the water lukewarm. Not cool, but lukewarm. I had no idea that I'd been cooking my feet! Now the pinkness reveals that the skin on my foot had died long ago.

Straightaway I call Sunaina, my daughter, who teaches

in a college in the city and lives with her second husband and two daughters.

I sense rather than see my daughter-in-law's ire. Ria wants me to call Sandeep, her husband, my son. But if I had called him, she'd go tch-tch, as if I was wasting his precious time.

Sunaina, I say hesitantly, I think the skin on my foot just came off.

Give me the phone, says Ria. 'Sunaina, it is nothing. Sandeep will be home soon. Then we will decide…yes… yes.'

'What did she say?'

'What? Nothing,' she smirks. She is always smirking. Of course, I have not had the pleasure of beholding her for too long. But from the wedding snaps and video, the first that I saw of her a year ago, there is the smirk. Like she knows something I don't. Even in sleep, and I saw her sleep purely by accident, the lips were in just that smirk. I wouldn't have believed it if I had not seen it. The ability to carry contempt that far into oblivion.

'Is she coming?'

'Who?'

'Sunaina.' We often have such conversations, winding nowhere, like short pieces of string.

'Why should she?'

Yes, why should she, I thought. The last time she came Ria read a mag while Sunaina made tea for all of us. Ria says the maid cannot, in all fairness, be asked to cook as she is there just to look after me. Good help was hard to find and if the maid fled, which no doubt she will one of these days because of overwork, oh dear, what would become of me?

So Sunaina had come straight after class and made tea and pakoras, which at first Ria said she did not want—'too oily!'—but later ate five of in quick succession. At dinner she complained to Sandeep that she was feeling uneasy, that the pakoras were just sitting in her gut like stone on stone.

'Darling,' he said in apology. That's all he says to her. She can say the plumber has to be called, that her sandal is broken, that the president is dead, and my son will say darling.

She looks at me when I am not looking at her. She does not know I know this or maybe she does not care. After all, I am an old man, and should line up along some shelf for perusal. It is not difficult to make out she is staring. When people are talking and all necks swerve towards the speaker, hers alone remains still; and when I look up I catch the end of her retreating eyes, the fall of lashes as if in the act of blinking. I don't know why she stares. Perhaps she thinks I will defecate in public.

The first gift she got me was a bedpan, the second a rubber sheet. Even Sandeep was rattled. He rallied around with, 'It is practical na, papa, to keep these things handy. We are family, there should be no pretences between us.'

I wondered what she'd do if I did crap on her sofa. There were the guests to be considered, the ambience, the sumo-wrestler candles lit up here and there, the tasty food from a good hotel and the sofa itself. Everything would have to be replaced, including the guests. Of course it will be cheaper to replace me; the thought *will* cross her mind.

'The sofa is no longer mine,' I have heard her shout once. Though the bedroom door was shut her voice carried. I did not hear the part before this, or after, so I was haunted by this headless ghost of an accusation—that sofa was no longer mine. Hers, she meant, hers. That the sofa used to be hers and was no longer hers. Then whose was it?

I had scuttled away guiltily from the sofa immediately like a crab. It was a fact that I had gotten fond of that sofa. Why? I have no idea. True, it was huge, warm, soft to sit on, enveloping fully, but in the end it was just a sofa. Sometimes, I admit with shame, I lie down on it and go to sleep. I should've known it was hers.

Now naturally she was afraid I would soil it. As dusk fell I sat there on the same sofa, on which I sit without remembering her passionate declaration about its ownership…and then forgot to get up, slightly scared by the absence of pain in the exposed limb. My foot, the raw skinned one, I suspended over my other knee. It might get infected in this state if it came into contact with anything, I feared. Gangrene. The word danced inside my head into gibberish. I closed my eyes and napped a bit. It has become a habit to snooze during daytime on this sofa. Sandeep and Ria say I sleep all day. But what to do, I tell them, I don't manage a wink at night.

Night. Now that's a different story altogether. The joints ache, three out of ten toes feel like they are falling off, and whatever I ate or did not eat for dinner sits alive in my chest. Apart from the bodily discomforts there is also the polite way my mind crosses me. I don't get it, apparently, that the past is past and that this is the present and that the two have nothing to do with each other. I will turn over and expect my wife to be there trying to wake me up as she used to do, oh, so many years ago. Memories scatter back to front and I sit up sweating, heart beating fast, waiting for my mind to slow down and events to fall into place. Fifteen pieces of sleep in one night. Still, however wakeful I am, the alarm manages to jangle my insides every morning.

Ria goes into her room. Loud music follows. She always switches on the TV or stereo in her room when she talks on the phone. So I cannot hear. The old man is what she calls me, being the new woman.

I can hear her laugh. She has a distinct laugh. Not happy but sibilant, silly with a lisp. Of course the music could also mean she is with her laptop. Which has something called a hard drive that stores everything. Everything! Can you imagine that? This memory can crash but can be retrieved, for though her hard drive has crashed many times, she says she has resuscitated it effortlessly on each occasion. Maybe, I had replied, it doesn't want to remember.

It was Sandeep who got me the walking shoes. So I began to walk. That is, most evenings I cross the road, look to the left and to the right until my head feels dizzy, get in through the park's side gate and hobble up its length once or twice. The thought of returning home and facing her spurs me on to more rounds. Here I also run into other old men from my building and we stand there talking about the good old days, when we were not so old. It gets difficult to remember who's lost his wife and who's not. The only thing in the present tense is our pension, its increment, its delay, and the desolation and disrespect that would have been our lot without it.

When I return home it takes me a while sometimes to remember. Remember anything. I have tried to study this and I can say that I am alright till I am in the lift. Usually one of my friends is with me and we say goodbye without a word of what awaits each one of us, what rarified form of neglect and punishment for going on and on like this. I step out of the lift…and I am lost.

Sometimes a child walks past, returns, takes me by the hand and leaves me standing before this door. Then I ring the bell, not because I remember, but because this seems like as good an option as any. See doorbell, ring.

Inside the house it gets worse. Ria often rearranges furniture, largely to accommodate her wrought iron pieces and the sofa. I know this, but when I re-enter the house I am surprised that the drawing room furniture is not the way it used to be during my wife's time. Ria sees me looking around and misunderstands. 'My tastes and talents go unappreciated,' she once told Sandeep, to which he replied 'darling'.

My memory tricks me all the time. The other day I began to talk to Ritwik Sharma before I remembered that we weren't on talking terms, not since we had that big row over parking space. Now of course we both don't drive.

Usually the drawing room TV is on when I walk in. It is Ria's way of reclaiming her space. Seated on a beanbag she'd be watching the news. This, if anything, further alienates me. War, floods, rapes, bombings—you can't run away; they will come and get you, ready or not. Even as I lower myself on to the sofa and dip my feet in water that I think lukewarm, the world locates me in my own drawing room and tells me such angry, foul things.

I didn't understand what my wife's open eyes were saying up until the moment she closed them because life had pulled its plug. It was much later when I myself lay helpless in some hospital bed that I understood what she had been trying to say then: 'Don't pull me back from the brink of death, prolonging my agony. I can understand why you do that, but you have to mourn my going if not today then tomorrow, and though my lingering postpones your own death, it doesn't, as you imagine, turn you immortal in the end.'

What did I want to keep her back for? And in what arrogance had I decided that this side of life was better just because I hadn't seen the other? She had by then glimpsed it, and it seems to me now that she pitied me my occupation of this side, that she looked back and saw me struggling to hold her life by holding on to her hand. Where she went hands and bodies meant nothing, that fly I kept shooing off her face meant nothing, my fear of loneliness even lesser. Living on and on is about hospital bills, ICU interludes and a medical allowance that never comes through. In the end it was not that I let her go, it was that she went anyway.

And, selfishly, I took it personally. I raged against her for days and months. I knew of course that she had a choice, that she had gently handed over a signed form at some counter that delivered her from our midst and unto another future. So I railed against her decision. Gone was the glass of warm milk at night. Gone was the single shared look, swift almost to the point of unmet. One by one, I tackled all of these and found to my surprise that I still miss her, to this day.

Then I began to envy her. For having left behind this tangled spool of insurance papers, troublesome digestion and heartburn that plague the living. She taught me not to fear death, so that soon I began to fantasize about my end. Will I charge towards my death bull to matador or go in my sleep smiling like a baby? I hope it is on a Sunday so no one has to take leave.

Ria picks up a bowl of fruit from the fridge and examines it closely, taking it to her nose to decide whether it is still edible or throwaway, whether to keep it or dump it. Oldness, it can be sniffed out.

When Sandeep walks in at 5 I close my eyes.

The first time he suggested I move in with him I had said no, no, I am fine. But then the transfer came to this city. Now he was in a bind. In the beginning he said the stay was only for six months. Now it is almost a year and no word yet from headquarters about a transfer back. The boss, who had come for dinner, said, 'Now I know why you don't want to leave here, Sandeep. Your family is here!'

Meanwhile the bulk of their beautiful furniture rotted in Ria's mother's place. The sofa and some pieces she brought here with her. The sofa I am getting too attached to.

So they live with me. Or people will say we have abandoned you, Ria says with that expression she adjusts to resemble other expressions. This incarceration then was one of those traps that spring out of the social nowhere. Soon the couple would fly away into the yonder blue, but when no one knew.

It is better I pretend sleep when Sandeep comes in from work so that he can go straight into the bedroom which used to be mine before they moved in. I hear raised voices.

Sandeep comes out of the room with slumped shoulders. He was always telling me—without any prompting from me—that his wife was a bright little thing full of life. Maybe that is why he acted the corpse. Couples do tend to play opposites in the balancing act that is marriage. He switched on the TV and caught my eye.

'Ria must have told you...'

'Oh yeah, I forgot, his foot is a sight,' she said quickly, coming into the room.

What, said Sandeep. Then again, 'what?' as if we were talking on the phone and the connection was bad. The doorbell rang. It was a couple they knew: Rakesh and Minal.

Ria said, forget it, yaar, we can't make it.

'Arrey,' said Rakesh, 'what do we do with the tickets then? They cost a bomb. You were okay with it just an hour back when I called!'

'What to do, papa's foot is a mess. We may have to even take him to hospital.'

'Let's see,' Rakesh said, hunkering down. 'Switch on the light. Can't see a thing in this romantic lighting, man.'

Ria looked at Sandeep who switched on the tube light.

Oh my God, said Minal.

I know, I know, said my daughter-in-law.

This is serious, man. This is serious.

Sandeep bent to take a look. I saw his face blanch.

'It is nothing,' I said hurriedly. 'Looks worse than it feels.' It is true, there was no sensation in the foot at all.

The maid brought two glasses of water on a tray. Absently I reached out for one and then remembered it was for the guests. But Minal picked up a glass and pressed it into my hands and Ria said please, someone just drink it.

As I drank I felt an abnormal thirst take over. More, I said to the maid, who flounced off.

Forget the film, said Rakesh, let's take uncle to hospital.

It is my job, sighed Sandeep. 'Why must you guys spoil your day?'

I was feeling dizzy. I groped for support and sank back into the sofa. In the end, though I don't remember this too well, I think three of them went for the film. All except Sandeep. I think he and I went to the hospital.

SONS

The first thing you noticed when you entered Manka's house was this huge picture of Jimmy's—the one where he was trying to smile with his lips shut, as a front tooth had 'died and gone to heaven'. You noticed this straightaway as it was right opposite the front door. The police, relatives and the vultures from the press, they all noticed it first too. They smiled politely as if Jimmy was dead and she his mad believing mother.

Sometimes Manka, bored by their queries ('Did he have access to drugs?' 'Was he beaten by his teacher that day?'), would gesture at the picture to divert them from the 'case'. They would have to look over their shoulders, since they always took the seat opposite her and she always sat facing him.

He came alive in those mud-splashed dungarees, in black and white unfortunately, to the immediate right of the door. A sweet portrait was next. From which he looked straight out, squeaky clean and cherubic, as if ridiculing anyone's right to think him dead. Above this was a small snapshot, framed in a hurry, of him leaning over a birthday cake with two candles. After the feasting that day, he had jammed her knickers—fished out from the wash—over his head, and run about like a mini warrior in a battlefield, embarrassing the hell out of her before guests.

On an antique table, which was part of her meagre dowry, sat Jimmy's favourite teddy bear, with one ear hanging by a thread that she refused to stitch back, so that he would find it exactly as he had left it. But he would be less of a child and more of a man by now and want to have nothing to do with teddy bears, with or without ears.

At first Manka thought the stream of visitors with their tragic expressions would never end. The police, who had initially come in with a swagger intended to intimidate, said various things at various times to cover up their inefficiency. Each theory they put forth was different from the last, you had to grant them that.

'It is a kidnap,' they charged in. Where were the phone calls?

'He has run away.' When he had a birthday party to attend that evening? Not bloody likely, like Joe would say.

'Could be kidney traffickers.' His were too small.

'Murder.' The body?

'Why don't you opt for adoption?' Clara, Manka's aunt by marriage, had asked in her usual well-meaning interfering way. But Manka had demanded that exact angle of eye, diameter of smile and distances between facial features as Jimmy's.

Once upon a time, in a bedroom far, far away, when Manka was newly married and the breeze held no foul breath, divorce had been a fashionable impersonal topic to discuss. Joe's tone carefully formal and his hands all over her, he had asked, 'You will still allow me access, I hope?'

He had been demanding conjugal rights when they would no longer be termed legally so, but was saying darling, I love your body and can't imagine ever falling out of love with it.

Manka heard the compliment only now, thirteen years after it was voiced, and when ties had turned soothingly platonic. Then she had told him seriously, 'I will marry again, so that will be impossible.'

He had not sensed that inherent dismissal of him then, indeed had thought her uncommonly witty. Gathering her close he had whispered against her breast as if into a mike, 'I can divorce you but never, never leave you.' For his courtship had not been without her permission, without her wanting to be wooed out of a broken heart. Manka meant daughter and she wanted to live beyond her moniker. Joe had come in quite by chance, and he realized it only much later, that anyone would have done. That generalizations had made an instance out of him.

Of course he did not need her in ways she needed to be needed. And the ways he did made not much difference to her. Not that the ways he needed her were in any way perverted or against the grain. He needed to escape tedious domestic details. She was the buffer between him and paperwaala, him and the washing-machine repairman, him and the vegetable vendor, him and the dressed chicken, the dry-cleaner. Though he never asked her if she liked to cook, it was taken for granted that she would do her best with all the stainless steel vessels waiting breathlessly on the kitchen shelves. He certainly did not need her to appear on the toilet seat, staring at him, talking to him, asking him to listen and talk back, while he shaved, showered and shuffled out most mornings.

Silence flowed easier between them now. Because eight years ago she lost her son. Eight years since she saw him last. She had put sugary-spicy doughnuts into his Mickey Mouse lunch box and he had waved at her from the window of his school bus. The bus turned a little to the left and then took that turn to the right that made it a yellow speck in the distance before vanishing from sight. That was it. He never came back.

The doctor had predicted three more hours of labour. 'Don't push,' they screamed at her, as the delivery table was too far. 'I am not pushing,' Manka had protested feebly. Attendants brought wheelchair and stretcher. But Manka, her labour too gone for such formalities, walked with knees bent sideways in Bharatnatyam pose, the hospital gown flapping open at the back like a pair of low wings, and had just managed to put her ankles into stirrups when out plopped Jimmy.

Ten fingers, ten toes, she prayed then. Ten fingers, ten toes, she prayed now.

She did not like to make a song and dance about her loss. But neither could she deal with it neatly, fold it away like the dhobi did the laundry in the building's garage. Manka could never stop looking up at a child's voice. *This could be him!*

She liked to think that she appeared to others like all the others. Those who never lost. Those who kept. She smiled. She wifed. She mothered. Till that day at least. She had conceived, multiplied, nurtured, nourished and loved. But loving was no effective prophylactic against losing.

Loss short-sightedly sank its blade into all those parts of her that really needed no introduction to scythes. Where job satisfaction was concerned Loss was particular about getting it right with overkill.

Manka never thought of herself as serene or composed. At nights, even now, she frantically swept her hand over the bed's middle to check for damp, still expected her son to wet the bed. She thought all could hear her teeth meet when children clambered over swings in parks. She wanted to smother their bonsai mouths with kisses, and while she was at it to strangle those bonsai necks. So she grit her teeth and took comfort in enamel demolition and cavity creation. One by one her dentist took out her chipped teeth and dropped them in a trash can along with bits of blood-stained cotton.

'These are wisdom teeth and not really necessary,' he would murmur into her rapidly thinning oral cavern, his hands busy manipulating the various mechanical ledges that hummed meaningfully. He also recommended a special toothpaste for her overly sensitive teeth. She felt a proper fraud for discussing her teeth with him when she had absolutely no control over the acid that spewed from her stomach to her mouth, corroding and contaminating all in its wake.

But even her dentist said behind her back that she was a calm patient, taking gum crisis in her stride.

૱

During her college years an increased preoccupation with academic pursuits had alienated Manka from the rest of her classmates. She had watched from a distance, alternately willing and unwilling to bridge the gap. It was Binoy and the effect of their combined hormones that redeemed her situation. With him by her side, Manka found she could participate without making those around her feel silly, without bringing them all down to her world of flat soda.

Cochin was too small a place to date discreetly and she had no compunction bringing her relationship into the open. Indeed she could not have flaunted it further when her parents began to clear their throats. Wedding date? Wedding date?

'My job is too low-paying,' Binoy said at first. 'My sisters have to marry,' he said next, since their own was to be an inter-caste marriage and would therefore nullify proposals for his sisters from 'decent' families. 'Let us wait till my promotion,' he said when his sisters were all matrimonially dispatched. 'I have a heart problem,' he said finally. He convinced her about his sacrifice and when she turned away, forlorn, placed a matrimonial ad for himself in the papers.

Wild grass snatched green blades into their wicked keeping and long stamens drooped helplessly under the sun's relentless rays. Droplets that started out kindly from the sun vapourized and lost their way. Boat trips to Bolgatty Palace were never one-way. The boatman waited patiently, boat tethered roughly in the shallow frilly edge of the backwaters, while his passengers—given to romantic impulses—combed the island. Manka fervently wished her boatman would disappear.

Film shooting was underway at a scalloped end of the island, she could see. A large crowd shuffled feet around a dozen garishly dressed matrons who were being taught to prance in an identical step. Ignoring the blare of a singular line emanating from the song speaker, Manka unfurled the sari from her head and bent towards some poor dried buds, letting the sun sink its teeth into her neck instead.

A cloud slow-motioned in the sky. She looked into the backwaters, so inviting their surface. She could jump, not go home. Or go home, not jump. This is sanity, she thought. To recognize choice. Manka laughed and immediately shut up. Two schoolgirls had wandered up, licking ice-cream cones. Their hot pink tongues darted around the vanilla, eyes surveying her curiously.

Manka had used up an entire packet of anticipatory tampons before the awful suspicion dawned on her. Could it be that her uterus was engaged otherwise? The urine test kit confirmed what the tampons said with their upturned tails. 'You can abort it,' the college campus doctor told her, his disgust evident in the gloves he remembered to put on before he delved between her legs, in the routine way he listed alternative methods of abortions.

Would he want to hear, in the middle of his busy schedule and sloughing off of gloves, the details of her dilemma? Would he appreciate the 'one-time' bit? A one-night mistake in a one-time hostel bed? That it was curiosity, a restlessness, a sense of adventure, even love. She had trusted. And lost. To an unmade bed and a hurried coupling. And it had been only that one time.

The soreness alerted her when she came to. She had trusted again. And lost again. To another unmade bed and a hurried decoupling. And it had been only that one time.

Manka glanced down at the waters again, at their solace and depth. But the boatman had of course waited.

Joe had come along, and she'd found herself breathlessly agreeing to hold an orchid bouquet, wear a fake tiara and fat gold ornaments flattened for maximum effect, to cutting a three-tiered cake, to fidelity, motherhood and everything else for better or for worse, in sickness and in health, till death did them part.

She hoped he had a magic wand that would make her forget Binoy's betrayal, stop her tearing her saris length-wise in the middle of the night to test their strength: *can it carry my weight?* Her mistake really. Expecting the universe to backtrack. As if sweet nothings were scientific facts.

Kamlabai spent long moments untangling the knots in Manka's hair, wetting it, blow-drying it, French-plaiting it.

'You have to apply oil all the time,' advised Kamlabai. 'See my hair, I henna it also. You! You are using shampoos. And then? It comes away like this.' She held up a small ball of hair procured from Manka's scalp triumphantly.

Manka, watching herself and her impromptu hairdresser in the dressing-table mirror, couldn't bring herself to deliver a lecture now on the role of greens and genes in the life of a healthy hair. She was too busy fighting new sensations. After...after what had happened, she had never dared to leave the house. Once when she tried to go to church she found she couldn't. Her knees wouldn't budge, her hands trembled, her feet stuck out all wrong.

It was only after she decided not to go that she breathed easier. Then she had stood at the window ledge, peeping down at people. Just people. Down below. Carrying on with their business. Walking purposefully or leisurely strolling to and fro. She felt safe as long as they couldn't see her. But to actually be there, amidst them, walking alongside… Manka balked at the idea.

Now, with husband by her side, she was taking the plunge again. Into people. Into the world they inhabited. Into the territory of loss again. It was New Year's eve, after all.

By and by she was bewildered by the ease with which others referred to her. For so long, with nobody addressing her except the prophets of doom—the police, the press, the doctors—she had believed in her growing invisibility. Till Jimmy surfaced she had agreed to slowly erase herself. Now it pleasantly disturbed her that she had not wished herself away. She was still there, solid as ever, evoking comments, conversation. No one accused her of being a non-mom, of faking maternity. She stood very much apart from the birth and misplacement of a son, as a woman, any woman.

She still had to take it all in.

It had been a messy process. To untangle the matted hair. But undo she did those rough braids.

∽

Manka crossed herself and sat down carefully, too exhausted to stand in church. Hand on heart she felt split into two. Her body sighted benches and plonked down promptly but her mind—the remaining rational bits of it—mocked her snail's gait and urged a faster pace. Now giving in, now tearing her heart out, her body rested while her mind propelled out of control. Today was Jimmy's birthday and she had decided to attend the Malayalam Mass. But it seemed she was too early. A choir group entered and began to practise hymns.

Over the altar a garishly painted Christ leaned, nailed hand and foot to the cross, as if to listen.

That baby wasn't meant to be. This one was. That one had come hurtling down the chimney. This one had come from her soul.

Manka tried to toss a sweaty strand of hair from her forehead. Why did churches all have such high ceilings? The fans were too far away to be of any use, plus their blades were still. Why should Jimmy pay the price for his sibling's mistake, of having come too early into their mother's life?

Everything about Jimmy's arrival had been so perfect. The marriage, society's patient wait for her pregnancy, the nine months, the handing over of baby after due registrations. That other baby, he wasn't meant to be. He was an unripe fruit

Say ta-ta, Jimmy. Wave hand like this. Manka waved her hand, attracting the attention of the choir who waved back.

Loose prayer leaflets flew down (the fans were now on) and the early evening sun was arranging shadows within steeples. Manka slumped back, idiotically at peace. Had she really thought Jimmy hers? When she had conceived him selfishly, senselessly, to assuage her sense of guilt, when she had not wanted him for the man she had borne him with… There had to be a bliss connect.

Only pure passion can purchase pardon. And when there *had* been that she had mercilessly killed the child, snapped its tender neck on medical advice. That one was meant to live. How dare she tamper with the divine masterplan? That is why Nature had devised the coming together of two mates in the first place. It was all in the mating, not the method. So here she was, no more randy, no more ripe.

When Binoy had tossed aside the fierce loyalty that had twisted her heart all out of shape it had been a season of the sun. Blazing hot, dappling the backwaters and burning up the green plantain leaves to a crisp. But that was a summer gone, a summer done with. It had been a lazy vacation month when the night sky popped dark stars like mustard seeds. When fence-less, park-less lovers had been the norm and goodbyes were dealt with sundered souls and joined hands. With a hundred 'nos' and a single 'yes'.

When Jimmy disappeared, the weather bureau had assured 'no rains'. Manka had turned herself over to the unbearable warmth. This was a summer with unfinished business. A summer that stored more heat around the corner.

Now in keeping with her husband's mood the rains were here, plastering hair, pinning thoughts, drenching all. Joe was guilty of cheating on her. And she was guilty of having pushed him into it. This longing of his for another woman, she was behind it, was she not?

She was the woman he wed, the mistake he made. Only dull-null women like her could make the other woman look flamboyant, their placidity rendered the latter a comet. Next to a watered-down wife anyone is flammable, someone to want. Only to this new woman whose sole claim to him lay in her newness, in her not being the wife, he could gripe all he wanted about being a husband.

While that woman dreamt of carrying his future babies and going for picnics with them one day, she herself could only stack up pictures of a child there used to be.

A child who had demanded the denuding of the heart, which continued to beat, exposed. This was but a specific detail of loss. No, she had no interest in looking into the whites of her spouse's eye and finding a new focus for the body. But that had nothing to do with love or a lack of it. It was merely that in her house living had been put on hold.

Manka went down on her knees and drew the sign of the cross.

On the way she saw small children in the park, clutching their mothers' fingers.

'Chalo Baba black sheep bolo,' a woman said.

'Mommeee...'

'He knows it fully,' the woman said, delivering a blow to the child's head. Then they all noticed Manka. She could feel their eyes settle accusingly on her back.

'Baba black sheep, how many, how many? Wool?' the child's voice questioned. But Manka knew the women. *Murderess*, they were thinking. *How can anyone misplace a son?*

Back home, having wiped all of Jimmy's pictures, Manka finally faced the TV. Like a tired warrior who surrenders before a powerful enemy, she switched it on.

NIGHTS

He comes to me in the night, shutting all doors behind him, letting me weep all over his chest, saying shh in the nicest way. Then we sit on the bed holding hands, and though all day I think only of what to tell him, there is no rush of words. If I do not lie back, I know he'll spend the entire night just looking at me.

My touch is a bit desperate because twenty-four hours will have to pass before I meet him again. His breath is like the five elements at once: earth, ether, water, air, fire. Even as I despair, I exult and reach for him again as this is all we have. It is difficult to maintain satiety with the knowledge of his departure hanging between us.

I only vaguely know his identity, his everyday public life name and designation. It would only raise disbelief if I let on the truth, that he—of all the men in the world—is my lover. I can see the laughs, the taunts, even the envy wrapped in cotton-wool compassion that will come my way.

Crassly enough, I met my second husband through him, but the nocturnal visits came much after that, after my remarriage. Before that there had been a limbo, two to twenty months of nothingness. It was in my third month as a bride the second time round that he came secretly, deliciously. From then on, my nights were his.

Between hungers, we sleep like babies. Sometimes I cling, towards dawn especially, suddenly terrified that he won't return. Why should he? What is there to return to? And all the goodness in society will never accept this relationship.

But the words won't come out and I start to shake. He, too, is wordless as he hugs me and strokes my back in long gentle sweeps that lull me back to sleep. When I wake up he has already left.

There are dark shadows under my eyes and as I pour out the juice for my husband's breakfast, he remarks upon them. 'Bad night?'

There is nothing he won't do to get me rested. My nerves are a talking point for his whole family. They make me tea, involve me in small manageable jobs and then worry that I am still so detached. You have to make an effort, his mother tells me as I tap a foot, waiting for the night.

I wish we—he and I—were far away from here, in the land I grew up, which my parents had to leave in the dead of night in order to keep living. It was a small house, I remember, but ours. There was a grandmother and grandfather (stubbornly they did not leave with us that night and therefore could not keep living) who are still there in my imagination. And in that little kitchen garden, amid the tomatoes and mint leaves, I hold out my hand and he takes it. We speak in Urdu and another language wholly ours. But I remember what my father said to me on the night we fled, 'Everything ends, even the night.'

As night approaches I grow anxious. I bite my lip, I am jumpy at a party that I have thrown. I am nodding my head but also shaking it. I want the evening to end, to wrap myself in two arms of my choosing. Also, after my husband goes to sleep, I have to unlatch all the doors, every single one of them or how will he enter? I worry about that.

While I wash off stale breath with soap, my husband stares at me strangely. Nowadays I brush my teeth twice in the night and change nighties at least once. It is the sweat, I tell him and he nods quickly, understandingly. This abstract kindness sets my teeth on edge. If you think I am mad, tell me, I want to yell at him. But I say nothing, just try to sit still and wait.

I am breathless. Fretting does not help, doesn't bring him any faster. I stare at the clock, wishing it to abracadabra. I take off the delicate clasp from my hair, careful not to wake my husband whose mouth is slightly ajar in sleep. My hair is now loose about my face, my breath sweetened. I arrange my limbs as if for a photograph. These small preparations are necessary or they will look deliberate after his arrival. I am vain enough to want to look my best without appearing too bothered about it. To smell nice too. To wipe out the toothpaste from my mouth. To smell of only me to him so that I can smell of him.

The sound of a footstep startles me though I strain to hear nothing else. You came, I turn to him. Don't stumble, I entreat even as I want him to hurry into my embrace. Your face, he says, is of such brightness, it turns night into day. I shush him with my hand on his mouth. I want him to notice my husband on the bed and be careful and quiet but he doesn't and soon I forget, too.

There's a world out there to be explored and no man or woman can do this alone. This world needs two travellers. He and me. Only together, as a pair, as a couple, can we set out to discover it, marvel at it.

He bends to kiss me, lick me, nip and nibble me before I can make the request, before I can beg and plead and break into a million pieces of want.

His tongue, faintly damp, touches mine. His teeth leave a mark now and then, but I am ready with the excuses. This red spot? A bee sting. The sore? God knows. Sometimes a shrug is more useful than to be all-knowing about every single mark that befalls the body.

We never talk about our earlier life, the two of us, as we reach out for each other, blissfully blindfolded by each other. The life before they all came to me, his friend now my husband, and said your husband is dead. Dead! For a long time after that I sat motionless. At least I do not remember moving. His body, naturally, they never found and there was no funeral. Missing in action, they said, as if I'd fuss about being denied posthumous emoluments.

Don't you see, I told them, there can be no pyre as long as he lives. He is dead, they kept repeating to me as if in therapy, as if wanting to see me defeated and weeping, to make me give up the reality of my life—of all those days and nights, of making plans and laughing and loving—that they said now belonged to the past...as if the past was less real than this and than them.

'He will never return,' that was how my second husband—the one who sleeps beside me every night like a guard dog—proposed to me, 'no use waiting'. I was lucky there had been no issue the first time, they said. I was too young and pretty to grieve forever it seems. Life—not life as I knew it or he knew it or as we knew it together, but another mysterious, unlived one in a shiny new foil—had to go on.

This marriage would help me live again, it will rid me of all the hopeless hopes that blanked my eyes. His family descended upon me, decorated me and told me many cacophonous moments later, that I was now married again, lucky me. Bewildered I watched my new husband's face get closer and closer...

Then the kindness, an onslaught I withstood bravely. Their mercy was borne like their lies, with equanimity, with a measure of goodwill and gratitude. An effort on their part and mine.

Until one night I decided to open the door and my husband—the first one as the others call him, the late one, the deceased one, the one at large, the one and only one really if you ask me—slipped right back in.

THE BITCH

'There is an alternative,' hissed the bitch inside Sara's head. 'And it involves the pillow.'

Sara stared hard at the pillow. It was encased in white lace, a gift from her mother-in-law on her first wedding anniversary. Where the lace was too fine, holes had developed.

'Oh, you didn't put them in the washing machine, did you?' her mother-in-law had exclaimed when she came to see the baby, careful not to sound accusing. 'These have to be hand-washed.'

Sara was given no time to defend herself as her husband's mother went back to the exciting game of 'divide-the-baby'. By the time she left, Sara's head was swimming with names of relatives who had apparently donated their features to the noble cause of beautifying her baby. There seemed to be little, if any, of Sara herself in the baby. She looked at the wailing baby, indifferent to its lack of resemblance to her.

All she wanted was the wails to stop and never return, so that she could snatch a few hours of sleep; exhaustion had made her boneless. But the cries were out of hunger, which meant she had to unhook the bodice of her maternity gown, uncork her nursing bra and let the baby's mouth wreak havoc with her sore parts.

Wearily, she gathered the newborn to her chest. The baby latched on greedily to its source of nourishment and all was temporarily fine. The phone rang, interrupting the baby's feed. Amidst his fury at the dislodged nipple, she managed to answer the phone on the third ring and absently reattach him.

'I am so excited for you,' the caller gushed. And Sara wondered if the job she had applied for a year ago had finally come through. Oh no, she means the baby, she realized in the nick of time.

'Does he have a lot of hair or is he bald like his dad? You are so lucky. Look at me, no baby till now.' The caller had an ultra-thin waist and a chirpy little voice.

'Yes,' Sara managed to croak.

'Anyway, as soon as Arun can make it we will be there to see the cute little sweetheart. Smooch him for me, will you? Bye.'

Sara replaced the receiver and planted no kiss on the suckling infant. Her bladder was too full. But that would have to wait till he finished his meal. She wondered what would happen if she suddenly plucked him off her chest and zoomed off into the bathroom. More cries, she knew. All the while that she bathed or ate or slept, he had only one agenda—to derange her. All this, plus the bitch taking up permanent residence in her head.

'How old is he?'

'A week and two days,' answered Sara precisely, without having to think.

'He doesn't look very big, does he?'

'A week and two days,' Sara repeated thinly, turning away to fold up the cloth nappies at the foot of the bed. Her husband had gone to the kitchen to make some tea. His boss was paying them a visit.

'Both my kids were heavy babies. Like Sumo wrestlers. Ha ha.'

'Ha ha,' she politely echoed as her husband walked in with the tea.

'I was just telling her about Tuppu and Puppu.'

'Who…? Yes, yes,' said her husband. 'They are really plump.' He looked at his scrawny son.

She thought, where is my tea?

The two men sipped from their cups and stared exaggeratedly at the baby. Then the boss made a preliminary attempt to 'hold' the baby.

'You must resent the hours he puts in at office on Sundays,' he said.

Sara was forced to nod again.

'Better a male heterosexual boss than a sexy woman to come between a couple, huh?' He back-slapped her husband, who laughed louder than necessary.

On the morning of their wedding anniversary he chucked Sara under her chin. 'We must make this a special night.' But she was fast asleep when he came in. The next morning he said it was a pity that she had been asleep and that they had not 'celebrated'.

The bitch bounded into her heart with a leap. 'Never mind,' Sara said. 'My father spent enough on my wedding day to warrant austerity on anniversaries.'

She had told him back then, shyly, as befitting a young virgin speaking to the man carefully chosen to deflower her on the wedding-bedding night, that she preferred a low-key marriage ceremony, where the focus would be on personalizing the occasion for her and for him. But he, his elder brother, his younger brother, his father and his mother had smiled politely with one pair of lips and said, no thank you. So that her father had to run from pillar to post borrowing money from friends who did not act like friends anymore, just so he could arrange her wedding.

Sara had wanted the occasion to be a seamless merging of her previous life with the future. That her virginity wouldn't carry a tag: 'offer valid till stock lasts'. She had rebelled against the demanded bullion—fifty fat sovereigns—weighing her down on her special day, but she had uncomplainingly carried all that metal nevertheless. She had wanted, no, *yearned*, that it would be a noiseless culmination of some grand cosmic plan hatched in the sky, that it would just be the tying up of loose ends.

She had certainly not wanted it to be the day that would separate the two halves of her life with a clash of cymbals. One lived and one she did not want to live.

'We must name him after his grandfather, of course. But what about his first name?' her mother-in-law asked, deftly refolding the laundry that Sara had just finished folding. 'So it will be XYZ Kurien.'

XYZ was not a bad idea, thought Sara, momentarily cheered. XYZ was exactly what her son felt like. Looked like.

'You don't have any name on your mind?' she asked again, more out of relief than any regard for her daughter-in-law's choice.

Sara shook her head. 'Sara' meant princess. Names meant nothing.

Later she methodically unfolded the neat pile of laundry her mother-in-law left behind. Sara knew her hair looked wild, as if thoughts leapt off her head and onto her scalp, causing static to lift the split ends. She bent closer towards the mirror. Yes, the strands were fairly crackling. Her husband hated her to cut her hair, preferring it waist-length, if not actually ankle-length, so he could run his fingers through it, sometimes painfully snarl them in it to manoeuvre her head this way and that in bed.

Really, did he have to invite all those people for dinner tonight? They were only coming out of courtesy to see the baby, after all. When she had grumbled, he'd said, if you can't cope, let's order in. So she said it was fine, that she could manage. She wished for once she could patronizingly gesture at the table and say that he had made it all himself. Or scowl at him when the baby cried or peed, and imperiously dismiss him to do whatever it was that had to be done to silence the source. Or to narrow her eyes at him in somebody's drawing room to signal an end to socializing, just like that.

'I know it's too soon,' he whispered late at night.

The baby had just gone to sleep after hiccupping a straight forty minutes. Sara's eyes were red-rimmed with lack of sleep and she vaguely remembered that she had not bathed today.

She secured her crackling hair with some pins and went into the kitchen to grind the rice and pulses, which she had soaked earlier. Thank God for dosas and idlis, they were easy to make once the soaked things were ground and mixed and left to sour and wait breathlessly for dawn in a pan.

Her father's letter that came this morning lay on top of the fridge. She saw it when she refrigerated leftover curry. She briefly considered showing the letter to her husband, of sharing the fleeting happiness she felt when it came, the news therein...but knew she wouldn't. Long time since she met her people. Her parents were too old to travel for the christening, only her brother planned to come. She had wanted to go home during her confinement, but the doctor and well-wishers had thought travel would put undue strain on her and the baby. Her mother did not come either, adhering to some old-fashioned notion about being a 'guest' at a married daughter's home.

It was not just her parents she missed. There were the familiar neighbours, old friends, cousins, aunts, her home, her room. The whole 'unmarried' routine that had been so different. But her world was changed now. When she went back it would be as the 'married' daughter, even if her husband did not accompany her. And here in this house she was yet to feel at home though she had hung her favourite watercolour on the wall and kept her books alongside his on the cane shelf.

She wanted to tell her husband that she would like to go home after the christening. But not today. She was too tired and the baby would wake up soon. Sleep had to be clocked while it slept. That is what the doctor had told her. 'Try to time your naps with the baby's.'

When she re-entered the bedroom she wasn't looking at the baby, but still sensed its movement. A tiny hand fluttered, hovered uncertainly in the air and then returned to the bed. Sara froze. Her hands clenched into fists. She was sure he would awaken now. But it was a false alarm. Mildly resenting the fright he gave her she turned to the bathroom. The smell of baby things had transformed it into a stranger's bathroom, but she nevertheless washed her hands, brushed her teeth.

Her husband had switched off the main light, meanwhile. Now only a small, dim-watt bulb was on. This was again for the baby. So that when he woke up in the night, as he so often did, he wouldn't be too startled. So that he could visually locate his victims and rip into them with those man-sized howls.

Sara walked towards the bed. The baby was still asleep, the manually disrupted end of his umbilical cord moving up and down in rhythmic abdominal breathing. Thank God for disposable diapers, thought Sara, primed to faint into the abyss of sleep, when her husband turned around urgently, her nipples his rosary beads, saying, 'I know it's too soon, but it's been a long month for me.'

Not that Sara had missed the physical side in the least. Sometimes, she thought, it had been better that way. Instead of lying like a frog on a dissection table, thinking the brochure had looked so nice.

The bitch inside her head could never sit still. In fact, she had literally silenced Sara time and again by sitting up too suddenly. When Sara opened her mouth to reply, the bitch rushed in with a 'hello', so that Sara shut her mouth.

She was never quite sure how much the bitch meant to say and how much she herself spoke.

He mumbled about spending the night at his mother's house, which fell halfway between here and office. Even though this meant tending to the baby all on her own she was relieved. She would not have to watch hubby disintegrate during breakfast. He would pick up quarrels on the menu, on the crockery, on the cutlery, on the tablecloth. Sara could never win a single round. If the tablecloth was straight the tea was too sweet or not sweet enough, but usually too sweet because with unsweetened tea there was always the option of adding more sugar and not having to lose your temper.

The bitch hated to be woken up at nights so Sara had to deal with her and the baby at the same time. They both nagged at her, gnawing at her body and at her mind, pulling her leash this way and that. And the bitch always hissing, 'Pillow, pillow, you fool. Can't you put the pillow over that small screaming mouth?'

∽

The christening was scheduled for Sunday.

'I heard you are planning to buy me a sari,' her mother-in-law beamed coyly. 'I don't have one in purple. You know, in light purple, like, like…' And the rest of the day she kept pointing out to Sara 'the purple'.

The godparents held the baby, leaving Sara to slouch behind, arms dangling by her side. The priest blessed in the general direction of the crowd.

'There is Rene,' pointed out her mother-in-law. Rene had studied at IIM Ahmedabad and had once upon a time been proposed for her husband, a proposal disposed of by her academic pursuits. Now she stood there wearing a moss-green kanchivaram edged with golden mangoes and a coolly dazzling happily-ever-after smile. Sara noticed that the sari was tied low on the pelvic bone and the stomach was flat as glass. If you look closely, you can see her intestines.

You say that because your own waist is rot, lisped the bitch. The desire to slim down extended beyond physical issues as far as Sara was concerned. It was to hark back to a previous existence when she was not absolutely responsible for another human being. The buck should never stop with you, she thought.

Rene and Sara didn't speak to each other that Sunday. But Sara was conscious of all eyes upon the two of them, comparing and judging, aligning them on a single platform. The bitch was cackling. She lived for such moments.

∽

'I will make the chicken,' Sara announced.

This had been preceded by her husband urging his mother, 'Ma, make that flame-red chicken curry of yours.'

'Oh,' his mother protested with a modest, self-deprecating little laugh, 'I don't want to invade Sara's kitchen.'

'She won't mind. She is a tender little vegetarian really, aren't you, my Sara?' he had playfully squeezed her shoulder. Which was when she made the announcement.

There was a letter in the mail for her. A former classmate was getting married again. There was a handwritten note along with the card, 'I know it is a difficult time for you to come.'

The baby was becoming the perfect excuse.

Sara remembered meeting this friend a year ago, for another classmate's wedding. She had dark circles under her eyes and untamed curls escaped all around her head in an unaesthetic halo.

'Sara, I can't believe you did it too!' she had proclaimed as soon as they met.

She meant marriage, of course. During their student years, great things had been expected of Sara, she was reminded. 'And look at you now!'

I am only married, not dead, Sara had wanted to say, but that would have sounded such a bleat. So, instead she had concentrated on the dark orange outline on her friend's lips that did not begin to match the filling of lighter orange on the lips.

'I miscarried,' the friend moaned.

At such times the bitch would waltz into her mouth and on to her tongue, so that she made up an amusing story about her frazzled friend and narrated it to her husband on the drive back. She couldn't remember now whether he had laughed back then, whether the joke at her friend's expense had been worth the effort it took her to create wit out of somebody else's shambles—an alien mess that she had no intention of stepping in to straighten. She had also forgotten that the friend had the most beautiful smile back in college. Bracketed by dimples.

When Sara scavenged deep within she saw no reason for her unhappiness. Except maybe that she wasn't working. But that couldn't be helped. She had to sit it out, patiently await the baby's weaning. Only, the baby seemed far too small, far too helpless. Far too much a stranger.

'Birth control?' the doctor asked without bothering to look up.

'I am breastfeeding,' Sara said pleasantly.

She lay there, her thighs trembling involuntarily in memory of the recent delivery when they had been brutally forced apart, and the copper-T duly inserted. Only, it did not suit her so that she bled copiously. Her husband met the doctor and came back with a note to wait and watch. So she waited and watched and bled. Then she dragged her anaemic self to another doctor who unhooked the copper-T and handed her some iron pills, which immediately constipated her.

In the waiting room a young mother spoke without preamble. Something about small babies made frankness fashionable. Like carrying little icebreakers in your pocket or pram.

'Does your husband help?'

'Doesn't yours?' asked Sara, striving for a workable honesty herself.

'No, I mean he is happy with the baby and all that. Doesn't think it is the milkman's. But he pounces on it like men do on their wives. You know, when it is sleeping peacefully or playing happily. Then he will carry him on his shoulder, make faces at it. But when it is crying or cranky, it is all mine. It is like the baby came out of me so it comes back to me.'

∽

'You know, you are not normal,' he declared, specks of scrambled eggs taking a detour to his chin. 'It is like someone has zipped up your mouth. You are not normal.'

She already knew that. Had just demonstrated as much when she went on pouring water into his glass even after it was full and the water ran out on the table, over her feet and on to the floor.

'There is something wrong with you.'

She kept the jug down. The water was over. And then she laughed. It was like a dam had burst inside her and all the mirth, which had been locked up inside her narrow skeletal confines, escaped with a snort. And while she sat rocking herself, cracked up by invisible wit, her husband looked scared for the first time. He had felt faintly victorious when he had accused her of being abnormal, but now he was apprehensive. Why was she laughing? What was so funny, dammit? But he dared not voice the query. That afternoon he called his mother.

Sara was rinsing the nappies when his mother bustled in. She stood at the doorway and rustled the curtains. 'Are you alright?'

Sara, who had been kneeling on the bathroom floor, slowly got up.

'Where is the baby?'

Sara walked out to hang the nappies in the sun to dry. When she returned her mother-in-law was clutching the infant and looking at her with wide eyes.

'I am taking him home with me,' she said.

Sara switched on the radio.

Without the baby in the house she began to miss people. The bitch was no great company either now that the baby was no longer around. Sara sat on the rocking chair and watched excess milk dampen the front of her dress.

He came at last, but he did not hook a leg over hers and murmur it had been a long time. Instead he asked her strange questions. Did she know that the flat was in joint names? Was she prepared to go away quietly or did she intend making a fuss?

Go away where, she wanted to ask. But he never allowed her to complete a single thought. She watched bewildered as he walked around, fingering the TV, the fridge, even the juicer and telling her over and over again that they were all technically his. Then he turned to her and softly, menacingly, he enquired, 'Aren't they?'

She did not understand, but some latent fear had her say yes, yes, they were.

∽

The room they gave her had no windows. In fact, the walls were padded so that she could not hurt herself even if she tried. Sara tried to bite her nails but they were already chewed down to bare minimum. She craved only the tiny pinprick of pleasure that would set her free to roam new and distant shores where she floated on the waves of unformed, hazy thoughts, with both hands free.

HAPPY

It was when she was almost seventy that she began to ask what women wanted, more as a question to herself, old enough to know that questions come from anywhere but answers lay within. What do women want? And what she came up with at the end of a hotchpotch dissertation—filled with flashbacks and selective memories, and all the books she read now only two lines in her head—was a gender-specific one (if only for the fact that she's been a woman all her life and in no mood to change that).

The average woman only wants to be happy. Seventh heaven, cloud nine, upbeat, in high spirits, on a roll, stairway to heaven, fool's paradise… Any of these will do for permanent address. To be happy no matter what, where and when, against all odds, relentlessly, repeatedly. If one can be butcher, businessman, nun or novelist, why not plain happy? People pursue PhDs and outer space, so why can't one aim for excellence in ecstasy?

Here, in this sepia photograph, her small hands are wide open as if formally addressing the world from her father's lap. There is another, a class snap, in animated chat with the girl to her left, and she can almost hear her own voice.

Daddy's girl, teacher's pet, mother's little helper. Born with a soluble sachet in her stomach that dyes her moods bright. The ribbon in her plait flaps in the air as she spins.

Growing up, she measures happiness by tackling her figure first and foremost. One is not tall enough, thin enough. In the war with morsels, food wins, uneaten. Once she learns to live with hunger, she is re-happy. When she is alone, she runs her hands down a narrow waist and compact hips—her body, all hers!

And despite the reality of ambiguous, indifferent, raised-voice unions around her, she decides, in a moment of impossible hope, to have the perfect wedding to the perfect man and live a perfect life. It is considered a womanly thing to maintain harmony and matching cushions, amiable smiles and a world-class menu. She quits her job, not because anyone asked her to, but to focus on happiness full-time. To wake up with nothing to do but be happy, happy, happy. Oh, how she was going to be happy! Off on a honeymoon they go, happy she and happy he.

Ah, here they are, in an entire album of wedding pictures. She in red, and mostly with his mother, who stands so close to her it is impossible for the photographer to get her alone.

She knows without being told that she is to be a foil, a backdrop, the fulcrum, nucleus, the hub and hibiscus in this alliance. In the mornings she is chirpy and cheery as she waves him bye. Briefcase in hand and pen in pocket, he sometimes forgets to wave back.

Man is to depend on, dance to. She prepares to coo, to soothe, to sponge-bathe his brow and smell nice. It is his right as a man to be grumpy. Late evenings when he is home with shoulders drooping, she grows more vivacious in her effort to merry-make. Not so much jolly as sunny, eternally buoyant. Like the fizz that hits the nose when you open a soda. She suspects it would make his day to see her down for once, this tiny bird who cheep-cheep-cheeps.

It makes her happy to make him happy and he is not happy with so much. If she corrects this, tweaks that, recharges, changes, modifies, alters, redoes, rethinks, rewinds, he hints he'd be happy. And this of course would make her happy. That goes without saying.

She twists her ring, the forever on a finger. Two kids later she is more determined than ever. Nothing is going to come between her and her happiness. Not the world or its naysayers, not the kids themselves who are more out and about than in and around. She enrols reluctant offspring for Bharatanatyam and badminton, plans surprise birthday parties, meets the woman who calls up one day asking to talk to her privately because long hours at work make an ass of most men. Husbands I tell you, her mother says.

Never-ending photos cascade down her hands—her kids dancing, on stage, playing sports, winning prizes, in fancy dress, crying, frowning, smiling—and for a moment she is buckled into a seat in the past.

Helpings of heartbreak would be the first to go if she could live her life in bits and pieces. Happiness would follow happiness and she'd live in a continuous revelry of joy. But with the sad bits gone, how will the happy bits live? Weeding out the sad from the happy would be an endless process.

Pull out less-sad, less-happy, lesser-sad, least-happy... Till only a handful of happies are left. And even these can be sifted through to find that one happiest. But how can the happiest survive in solitude? A more promising letdown will be harder to find with the saddest little happiest just here.

Here is a picture of her—the one her daughter has framed on a wall in her home, perhaps in preparation for when she dies—with the eyes she has today. When had her eyes changed so? Runny, like things cooked with too much water.

Into middle age happiness becomes the sensible kind. It makes sense to be happy since so many people depend on her happiness for their happiness: ageing parents, growing kids, family and friends. All those man-hours she put into being happy! (Or is it woman-hours?) Also, she can't be unhappy, it is a medical fact. Her tear ducts are gone. Sealed tight as tombs. Tears, from disuse, have dried forever.

Death and disease do their bit. Happiness becomes a necessity then, a weapon, the add-on starch to the limp cotton of her soul. She has to cling to happiness—to clutch and snatch at, and grab by the throat—even as it fights her tooth and nail. Happy, at this stage, is just blocking unhappy.

In old age, however, it is her ability to be happy in the future...say ten seconds from now, that she doubts. It is, she's afraid, a serious doubt. What if she can't convert a moment, any, to a better one?

Her daughter often said, 'I want a marriage like yours, for us to be happy like you and dad.' She looks at her husband, the bald diffused elderly man occupying the other half of her bed, and, really, he just happens to be him.

She doesn't remember when it was they stopped talking altogether. Maybe when she stopped talking about their son so he won't remember, and he stopped talking of their son so she won't remember, each doing their bit to sustain the happy, to ward off the unhappy. But now she allows herself to hold in her arms once more that little boy who was never meant to be, who sprayed upon them florally for a short, short while...

Her husband did not want to hear how the nurse gave the baby to her and the sight of their son the first time. And she did not want to hear technical details of the funeral, of the bill or those who forgot to condole or came without flowers and the sight of their son the last time. So they lay silent on the double bed, old-man him and old-woman her, and spared each other their ramblings.

Oh, how typical they'd become! Each thinking I am thinking of you, but thinking only of themselves, of having to go through one more day, of somehow getting through this never-end called life. When he was asleep, she'd turn to her side laboriously and watch him, wondering which was worse, him going before her or her going before him because—if she had a choice—why, she'd opt for what pleased him.

Death can take her anywhere it wants. How are you, she'd ask her son the minute she reached wherever he was. *Mommy's fine* is what she says every night before sleeping, *adjusting to a world with no you.* He had locked her in the bathroom once and she could hear him outside, giggling. She had knocked and called out, careful not to let her panic show. Open the door, she had said, open the door. She'd knock now till he did, and when he did she'd cuddle him, crying like she had then. And he'd run his hands over her face, saying, do mommies cry?

Happy is what was and what will be, never what is. Many an early hour she awakens absurdly happy, grinning like a madwoman, lost in a reverie from the past or dreaming something improbable, inappropriate. Senile but alive, life is all she has till she dies. Collating and recollecting instances of happiness. It is a drug, this happy. When the body can't produce its own it needs to be taken intravenously.

Trouble is, happiness is a noun. It smirks silently, invoking comparisons, disparities, the matter of more and less. Who is to say how happy one should be and what makes up happy and when is happy best? That, in all this military strategizing of contentment there are the here and now moments unasked for, unannounced. Like a sparrow sitting on a windowsill that flies off before she can look.

DAUGHTER

The dogs had stopped barking. With their tails tucked between their legs they cowered in corners among the debris. A brown pup was suckling its mongrel mother that lay stiff. Charu wanted to ask someone something. But he forgot what. Also, he did not know if he could speak. He tried to say aloud, 'Can I talk?' Though the wind had stopped howling through his hair, something still marred his hearing.

The market, where his shop once stood, was razed to the ground. Rubble and plaster covered his tie-and-dye hosiery stall. His face was streaked with dust and his clothes were ripped in the panic-stricken dash into the cornfields when he was jostled from all around. The tiny tricoloured paper flag on his kurta, though, was intact. Just this morning, while pinning it on his lapel, his daughter said, 'Babuji, can you take me to school on your cycle?'

'Have you forgotten it is Republic Day today? There cannot be school.'

'We are celebrating it in school with marching, babuji,' she told him patiently.

Charu's younger son burst in mockingly, 'You should see them, babuji. Left, right, left...like frogs!'

Before sibling rivalry raised its omnipresent head, Charu said, 'Yes, Munnu, we will go on the cycle.'

Someone touched his shoulder. It was an old woman. 'Please, can you pull out my grandson? He is in there somewhere,' she said in Gujarati. She pointed at a crumbling structure from which bricks and twisted iron bars had crawled out.

Charu vaguely knew that he should be mouthing comforting words, but all he could manage was a shake of his head. He saw her scrambling over to somebody else.

Slowly, still in a daze, he set out on foot for his home. The cycle, he knew, no longer existed.

On his way he tripped only once. Though strewn with rubble and concrete shards, he found it easy to climb up and down the uneven earth. Mechanically he trod on the newly unfamiliar path with none of the apartments he was used to seeing. Buildings lay on the ground, innards out. One such climb nearly toppled him over. He was sure the leg belonged to a woman. The ankle was slim and had a silver chain with tiny bells around it. He tried to walk faster, though the thought of what lay ahead made his steps slower and slower.

He reached Munnu's school. The once-proud building was now silent and prostrate. Charu strained his ears. No, no left-right-left could be heard.

He remembered how disappointed he'd been when told a daughter was born. 'A girl? Are you sure?' he asked his aunt, who was also the midwife in the family.

'Yes,' she had said, wiping her eye.

But that was before he met his Munnu.

He had thought the earth under him was going to tear open. First there were the vibrations, then it had begun to rock like a cradle. The wind had whipped the dust into a frenzy. All around him were cries of 'cyclone, cyclone'. The white tourists, who had been smudging his tie-and-dye merchandise with their unwashed fingers, had looked petrified. Then he heard the unmistakable crunching of stone walls that shook the very moorings of his heart. Like women possessed by evil spirits at temple festivals, he and the foreigners had made for the fields.

'It is a bomb,' another shopkeeper had whispered. 'Pakistan has done it.'

But even from a distance they could see the walls crack open, convulse and come down. Hands from the earth's belly were pulling them down.

He leaned against the broken-down school wall. His legs gave way and soon he was sitting by the wall.

Slowly Charu began to weep.

WORDS

Where do they go, words no one wants? No one uses anymore? When fathers die and mothers don't remember? All the love words and forever words and promises promised, pledges pledged and vows vowed, when the mouth has moved on to other words, other people? Slips of the tongue and sweet nothings, *baby* and *bitch*, killer lines and jokes that fall flat, all in the Orphanage for Words. For words once spoken have to go someplace.

Words spoken to be seen. Words said for they had to be said. Those that couldn't be said because they shouldn't be said. What one wants to hear, what one is made to say. What one refuses to hear, what one will never say. Retracted, regretted, rebutted. That live too long unsaid, a fourth-stage-cancer word. And words that go ahead and say themselves.

A thousand secrets make the body a bow but the arrow shot from its mouth is always a word.

Small talk. Big talk. Dirty talk. Pillow talk. Bilateral talks. Baby talk. Body talk. All talked out. Talk to me. All talk! Talked into. Idle talk. Locker-room talk. Talk down to. Talking shop. Let's talk it out. Sleep talk. We have ways to make you talk. We need to talk.

Folk tales and fairy tales, myth and fables, anecdotes and reminiscences. Four-letter words and famous last words. Said behind your back, told to your face. Last text from an ex. And words totally reversible–'I do'–because no one 'does', not really, not for long.

Wedding vows, divorce documents. Straight from the heart, off the cuff. Old wives' tales, euphemisms, slang. Nothing but the truth. Said in passing. Say it like it is. Itty-bitty utterly-butterly baby-faced words. Barely audible. Bandied back and forth. Banter, backstabbings. Going-through-the-motions, everyday, you and me words. It's the liquor speaking. A word of advice. Fuck-me words in killer heels.

Breaking news. No news is good news. Hey, what news? First, the good news.

Let me tell you a story. The story of my life. That's a whole other story. Tell the story properly. Story so far. Cock-and-bull story. A sob story. The inside story. Cover story. Moral of the story. Coming-of-age story. Bedtime story. To cut a long story short. What's your story? Back story. Story behind the story. Let's get our stories straight. His side of the story. Stick to your story. Likely story. End of story.

Star-crossed Romeo-and-Juliet words. Whistleblower words. Wikipedia words. Rumour has it. On the same page. Chapter and verse. Shoot the breeze, chew the fat. Nineteen to the dozen. On second thoughts. What you say when asked, 'Was it good for you?'

You have a point. Beside the point. The point is... Point taken. Point for point. Point to be noted. Come to the point. This is pointless. What's your point?

Can you keep your word? Give your word? Go back

The Orphanage for Words 171

on your word? Take my word? Your word against mine. Just say the word. In a word. An exchange of words. Word for word. Have a word with him. Word of mouth. Lost for words? Don't put words in my mouth. Take back your words. A way with words. True to his word. Click on this word. A word or two. Word for the day. Run out of words. Put in a word for me. Word count. Wordplay. Don't breathe a word to anyone. In other words. Mark my words. There's a word for it. My word! Last words. Eat your words. Words aren't my thing.

FYI. FIR. PTO. OMG. BTW. TMI. TBA. LOL. TTYL. SOS. WTF. FAQ. BS. PS. www. #.

We regret to inform you. Let me run it by you. I tell you! That came out all wrong. I'll tell you about it sometime. Hello, can you hear me? Your voice is breaking. Don't take this the wrong way. I didn't mean it like that. Just between you and me. Thank you for asking. Don't call us, we'll call you. That's not what I meant. Even as we speak. Don't ask! *No one speaks to me like that, no one.*

Music to my ears. Make a song and dance. Sing for your supper. Blowing own trumpet. Set to music. They are playing our song.

You have the right to remain silent. Blank calls. Pregnant pauses. The long and short of it. Public announcements. Come straight to the point. Cut and dry. Words that are crannies, cul-de-sacs, hills alive with the sound of music. Dénouements. Misspelt, broken, accented. Start at the beginning. Contested wills. In full flow, placating, flat, flute-like. Going gaga, gush gush gush, hyperbole, bling words, tall tales, size-zero words all the rage but mean nothing nothing nothing. Cliffhangers. Spoken but unheard; heard, not spoken. Easier said than done. Rejection letters and pink slips. Confessions. Eulogies and obits. Double meanings. Endearments. Flattery. Fine print on shampoo bottles. Generally speaking. Verbal diarrhoea. Bang on. Tall claims. Promises, promises. *Papa, don't!*

Every single password in all the PCs on the planet, all the unsaved files. Spam, forwards and chain letters. Dear Sir, Dear Ma'am, Warm regards, Yours sincerely, Thanking you.

No question of it. Good question. Does that answer your question? Question time. Any questions? The question is how. Out of the question. Can you repeat the question, please? A loaded question. No questions asked. A question of time. Begs the question. The question doesn't arise. Trick question. Ask me no questions, I tell you no lies.

Fifty-pound weakling words that get sand kicked in their face. Addled, acidic. Get if off your chest. Blow hot, blow cold. Hissed. Hue and cry. Passing the buck. For argument's sake. Rantings and ravings. Pure bluster, hot air. Doublespeak. The medium is the message. Don't shoot the messenger.

Many a slip twixt cup and lip. Malapropisms. Freudian slip. The stammering fan asking for autograph. Calling a bluff. In conclusion. Jack-in-the-box words, words that jump out from behind a sofa screaming 'surprise!' Lies that men tell women to get them into bed. Lies that women tell the men they are cheating. The bad, bad poetry of first love. And the dead serious, 'You don't mean that!'

Dear John,
On that note,
Speaking of which,
Icebreaker words, shape-shifter words. Replayed,

rewound. Punch lines. Words that belong in another sentence. Sugarcoated. May I repeat the order, sir? Words all over the place. Jack-the-Ripper words that pull out intestines naked in a bed. Frankly actually basically personally.

Did I just say what I just said? I don't know how to say this. As I was saying. I will say this just once. Say it with me. There, I've said it. Goes without saying. Just saying. Is it something I said? Say it to my face. Did you even hear what I said? Don't say it, don't say it, don't… You know what they say. What do you want me to say? You had your say. What did you just say? Don't make me say it. There's a way of saying it. So what you are saying is… I can't hear a word of what you are saying. What will others say? Saying the same thing again and again. Nothing you say makes sense. You were saying? Say something, say anything.

Money talks. Talk is cheap. Put your money where your mouth is. A penny for your thoughts. That's rich coming from you!

Pep talk. Frankly, bluntly, firmly. Cutting someone to size. Not a peep out of you. Now you tell me! Cheers and boos. Karaoke. And all the pet names you called the men you were in love with.

Empty promises, empty boast, empty talk, empty words, empty.

Dear Diary. Note to self. Tweeted, texted, typed, deleted. Writing on the wall. Code words. A sales pitch. A blow-by-blow account. Chants and spells. A gabfest. Intelligence reports. In requiem. Buttering up. Going around in circles. Beating around the bush. Words a lump in the throat. And words that jam your hands on the steering wheel long after the light turns green.

You really mean that? Milk and honey. Tongue-tied. All said and done. Say it again. Put like that. Well said. You don't talk to me anymore. Forget I said that. This doesn't change anything. Please hear me out. Where are you going with this? Listen to me. Don't tell me that. Telling tales. I digress. That's neither here nor there. It's all coming back to me. Opening up to someone. Harp on. Empty vessels make the most noise. Skirting the issue. Break it gently. I don't follow. Come again?

In the words of popular songs:
People talking without listening...
Words are flowing out...
It's only words...

Suicide notes. Message in a bottle. Approximations. Unrequited words: all dressed up, nowhere to go. Old yellowing letters at the bottom of a trunk.

Ask nicely. Talk him out of it. Making excuses. Don't change the topic. Let me do the talking. You don't open your mouth. Literally. Speak up, son! Spit it out. Something along those lines.

Matrimonial ads in second-hand magazines. Blessings from beggars at rolled-down car windows. What you say bedridden with lust. Said behind closed doors. Walls have ears. A single column on the back page of the last edition of a small-town newspaper. And words you hear between your legs.

Fighting words. Over my dead body. She asked for it. Pay attention! Fatwa. Meaning what exactly? I've heard it all now. Don't make me open my mouth. You don't know how to speak. Words can kill. Shut up! I hear you loud and clear.

The Orphanage for Words   175

Brainstorming. Think outside the box. Saints' sayings framed on walls. Rabble-rousing. Of unknown etymology. Lost in translation. That's Greek to me. What you tune out while tenderly eyeing your better half. Billing and cooing. What's trending. This won't hurt. Speak now or forever hold your tongue. And what can never be taken back in this lifetime: 'Happy birthday'.

∽

Words. Nuclear holocausts between clenched teeth. Heated exchanges in bedrooms/boardrooms/battlefields. A fang bursting its venom right in the mouth. Words small, medium, large. Two words running towards each other in slow motion. Offhand, fluff. The growing *'yes, yes, yes'* from the room upstairs. What dictionaries are crammed with. High pitch to low. Words to explain words, words to conceal words. Mother tongue. A foreign language. Fillers. 100 per cent literacy. Said in haste, jest, nostrils flaring, hands folded. A straight road from 'I love you' to 'It's not you, it's me'.

Stage whisper, sotto voce, inner voice, gut feeling, speaking in tongues. Nagging. Rhetoric. Yakkity-yak, jabber-jabber, tom-tom, chitchat, ad nauseam. Like hearing all the voices you've heard before speak at the same time. Melodramatic. Reducing to tears, ringing in ears. I said to myself.

Straight from the horse's mouth. Eating crow. Fishing for compliments. Barking up the wrong tree. The elephant in the room. Swan song. Sing like a canary. Old jungle saying. Gets my goat every time. Curiosity that killed the cat. Going ape. Huffing puffing wolves. Let sleeping dogs lie. Words that have you foxed. Butterflies in stomachs. Cat got your tongue? Crocodile tears. Don't rat on me. The cat's out of the bag. His bark worse than his bite. Words out of nowhere, like a rabbit pulled out of a magician's hat.

Open-and-shut words. Subtext. Tirades. A raised voice in the street. Ad-libbed. In parenthesis. Within quotes. What's bleeped out. At the count of three. In measured tones. Soliloquies and dialogues. A pow-wow. Lifting spirits. Saving souls. Breaking hearts.

Out of coverage area. *Parlez-vous?* Politically correct. Technically speaking. Condoling. Get a word in edgeways. Sub-words. Quotable quotes. With this bull I thee bed. Strings attached. Taking sides. Your first name and his surname scribbled together in your notebook.

The apt word. Raising a toast, dismissive, distancing, tit for tat. Muffled, matter of fact, ho-hum, what the hell. Words that stay long after the listener is gone, words that can't be recalled. Words that raise the fine hair at the back of your neck.

Free to chat? Out of context. Chat up a storm. A figure of speech, in a manner of speaking. Get it out of your system. My take on it. Honesty the best policy. Get it? The voice of reason. Tell me about it! Don't feed me a line. Parables and proverbs and pleasantries and platitudes. Words can't express. I can't read minds. A picture worth a thousand words.

Words that turn the tide. Misleading. Stories and scoops. Sage advice. Shouted from rooftops. Hushed up. The spokesperson said. Prattle. Bicker, baritone, blab. He said, she said.

The Orphanage for Words

Can you keep a secret? Hearsay, gossip, pssst. My lips are sealed. Me and my big mouth! Home truths. According to sources. Allegedly. You filled their ears against me. Stretching the truth. Spill the beans. In this ear and out the other. Somebody will hear. Shh...

Let's not go there. The less said the better. In a nutshell. Encapsulating. Tête-à-tête. Formulaic, clichéd, rhyming, inane. That's that then. Verbatim. Sound bytes. On the other hand. The oral tradition. Put that way... How do I put it? Imbue, infuse. Clear the air. Keynote address. Hit the nail on the head. Premeditated, artless. Fluent, fervent. Can't say no to you.

A white lie, a black tongue. Put it in black and white. Words that make you see red, make you blue, turn you green, pale you, are white noise or black holes.

Show, don't tell. Kiss and tell. Garble and gobbledygook, babble and gibberish. Echoed and parroted. Heated and frosty. Billed or gratis. Blurted out, said bluntly. Freedom of speech.

The plot thickens. Classic, bestseller. Unputdownable. To be continued. Not in the syllabus. Dedicated to. Bestselling, critically acclaimed. Sequel. First draft. By the book. Slush pile. Footnotes, glossaries, annotated. Pretty words all wrapped in a bow. First edition. Condensed, edited, abridged. Blurbs at the back of books. Once upon a time, far, far away, now an e-book with adjustable print. Twist in the tale. Printed, recalled, banned, pulped. Read and burn.

Words. Bitten off. Swallowed. A rolling of eyes. A pursing of lips. A wrinkling of nose. All ears. Put your foot down. A nose for news. You giving me lip? Lip service, lip-synced. Don't eat my head! Words with a finger on lips. Heart to heart. Save your breath. Bite your tongue. Foot in mouth. Words that go flying over your head. Tongue-in-cheek. Head nor tail. Out of the mouths of babes. An earful, a mouthful. There, on the tip of a tongue.

Where was I? I gave him a piece of my mind. Speak your mind. Speak for yourself. Spoken like a man.

Words. Pulsing on paper. Cupped in a palm like last water in a dry land. Coming out not quite right, thought before their time. Words struggling for breath, birth on. Their fate, to strain for a hearing.

Return to sender. Begged, borrowed, blah-blah-blah. Long-ago dialects. Words at the heels of words. Misshapen, guttural, nonsensical. Why kill one's own? Say and slay?

Arcing in the dark, the collapse of consonants. Words without windows. In a suicide pact. Red corpuscle words. Verbs adjectives pronouns. Travelling up throats from god knows where. Beheaded, tailless, twitching, on death row. Closing the door on the way out. A light year that has at last come to an end.

The unsupportable weight of what has to be said, put on record, signed. Publicly uttered. A turned back, resolute and stiff, the portrait of a spine held straight. The absolute *no* that slams a face shut. The insane axis of earth crashing through galaxies, breathing its last. Clasped hands undone knuckle by knuckle. Bottles after genies leave. Not a miracle more.

till. unless. until. wait, just wait.

Hinted at, implied, unsaid. A promise, a dream, taken as said. The almost-words. Pre-lingual. Virgins on wedding nights. Words from another mood. A finger drawing in the vapour on a windowpane. A solar system of syllables. Like a prayer prayed to listening gods.

What we try to forget. Bottled up. What psychiatrists shell like peanuts from our heads. Talking to yourself. Watching other mouths move as if underwater. A lyric scythed in two.

An old man holding his wife's hand in dementia. The exile of expression. Assassins of the present tense. Words yet to grow a soul. The sound of nothing to say. Like one mouth kissing. The ungolden silence of silences.

∽

Hush, little word,
in a shroud of tongue.
Unclaimed and mortal.
No floral casket.
Only mute hymns, mourners
Who tiptoe hands on ears.
Nothing more ear-splitting
Than a dying word.
Listen.

COPYRIGHT ACKNOWLEDGEMENTS

'The Cry' was first published in *Of Mothers and Others* (Zubaan, 2014). 'Mornings', 'Dog' and 'Doll' were first published in *Planet Polygamous* (Indialog, 2005). An earlier version of 'Happy' appeared in *The Economic Times* and 'Fathers' in *The Hindu*.